She was watching a miracle

This man's face was contorted in the agony of desire—desire for *her*. His face had become naked for her, hiding nothing. And she became lost, too.

All the human need and desire so long held in check by the barrenness of her life spoke to her. The long-buried sensuality within her came bubbling to the surface of her consciousness. Beth had been turned off to that part of herself for so long that its emergence frightened her.

But she wanted Jonathan Sky. She wanted to crawl inside him, to join her body to his, to merge her flesh with his and her soul with his soul. He made her want to believe once again that there was fulfillment in this life. He made her want to take that risk and find out.

ABOUT THE AUTHOR

As the daughter of an army officer, Indiana-born Anne Henry moved frequently during her childhood. Now she makes her home in Oklahoma, where she edits alumni publications at the University of Oklahoma.

Books by Anne Henry

These books may be available at your local bookseller.

Don't miss any of our special offers. Write to us at the following address for information on our newest releases.

Harlequin Reader Service
901 Fuhrmann Blvd., P.O. Box 1397, Buffalo, NY 14240
Canadian address: P.O. Box 603,
Fort Erie, Ont. L2A 9Z9

I Love You, Jonathan Sky

Anne Henry

Harlequin Books

TORONTO • NEW YORK • LONDON
AMSTERDAM • PARIS • SYDNEY • HAMBURG
STOCKHOLM • ATHENS • TOKYO • MILAN

Published October 1986

First printing August 1986

ISBN 0-373-16171-9

Printed in Canada

Prologue

"He was a great man, Mrs. Dunning," Jonathan said as he took his turn shaking hands with the slender woman dressed in a sedate black suit. Her hand was gloved in soft white kid. It was slender, too. Jonathan could sense its delicate structure beneath the leather.

She met his gaze with brown eyes—not the dark, almost black color of his own eyes but a warmer brown, like the eyes of the deer who used to raid his grandparents' garden back home in Clearwater.

Her look, however, was neither warm nor cool at that moment. In fact, the look in her eyes was remote, as though only part of her were receiving her husband's mourners and the rest of her had walled itself off from them. She was standing beside the impressive bronze casket, which would soon be lowered into the ground of the rolling hillside cemetery on the outskirts of San Diego. Even now, keeping a discreet distance from the proceedings, two overall-clad workmen hunkered down under a magnificent towering oak, waiting until the mourners finished giving final honors to the body of Justin Dunning, after which they could refill the hole they had dug in the earth.

"If there's anything I or any of the residents on the staff can do, don't hesitate to call on us," Jonathan continued as he gave up his hold of the woman's gloved hand. "I really mean it. Those aren't empty funeral words. I owe your husband so much. We all do. He was the most outstanding man I've ever known. I still can't believe he's gone."

"I know," the woman responded automatically, her words almost stolen away by the soft breeze that rustled the row of cedars behind her and gently played with a stray lock of her hair beneath the small black hat with a wisp of veil at the crown. A silly bit of a hat, Jonathan thought. It didn't suit her at all. Her hair should be loose and free.

"Back where I come from, we'd say at a time like this, 'I'm sorry for your trouble,'" Jonathan said, reverting to a bit of "down home" drawl as he spoke the words. "And I am. Truly sorry."

A small smile flickered across her face at his words. He had her attention now. Her brown eyes focused on his more fully. "Thank you. And I'm sorry for *your* trouble. How difficult it must be for you residents—to have your mentor taken from you in the middle of your surgical training. I know what a tremendous loss that is for you all."

How strange, Jonathan thought. Somehow their roles had become reversed. She was consoling him. He looked into the woman's face. It showed the strain of the past few days. She looked tired and pale, and the sunlight emphasized the dark shadows under her eyes. Jonathan tried to remember how she normally looked and realized he had no clearly defined picture of Mrs. Justin Dunning other than the quiet young woman he had seen a few times at the occasional hospital functions he attended.

Oh, he'd heard all those stories about how Dr. and Mrs. Dunning had met—how Justin Dunning had dramatically saved the young woman's life and later married her—but the legendary tale merely seemed part of the famous physician's mystique and didn't have much to do with the woman herself. Jonathan's recollections of her always seemed to have her standing unassumingly at her husband's side. He supposed he might have recognized her had he seen her without her husband, but the physical presence of Dr. Justin Dunning was so overpowering that he had overshadowed everyone around him, especially his young, soft-spoken wife. Dr. Dunning had always been treated with deference and awe by anyone he came into contact with, including Jonathan himself. Jonathan, when he was in a room with Dr. Dunning, was so aware of him and so intent on listening to the great man's words, hoping to glean insights about his surgical techniques or his philosophy of medicine, that he was oblivious of anyone else.

Dr. Dunning had been recognized for almost a decade as one of the world's leading heart surgeons, and he was revered by his patients and the media, who had long ago found that the larger-than-life Justin Dunning made good copy. While he was California's version of Texas's Michael DeBakey, he also represented the next generation of heart surgeons. Besides, he was even more controversial, and he photographed better. The two heart surgeons were often compared. Jonathan recalled having watched one television special that was called *Dunning and DeBakey, the Demigods of Heart Surgery*. An article in *Newsweek* on the two men had been headlined "The ABC's and two D's of Heart Surgery." More recently, Dunning had been the one getting the most attention. Dunning, the miracle worker. A maverick. An outspoken critic of conservative medicine. A prophet. Tall and handsome, with a mane of graying black hair and piercing blue eyes. Wherever Dunning went, the media followed.

They were all there today with their cameras and notebooks. Even in death, Dr. Justin Dunning was news. The whirl of television cameras provided accompaniment for the multispecied chorus of birds that were impatiently waiting in nearby trees to reclaim their quiet domain. And what a dazzling group of California's famous and near famous had gathered for the media's cameras to capture. Many of the mourners owed their lives to a Dunning operation. One former patient, a deposed Middle Eastern monarch, had flown all the way from Switzerland to attend the funeral and was accompanied by two wives in traditional dress. There was a former baseball great turned television personality. There were film moguls and Hollywood stars, including the aging but still debonair entertainer who had sung and danced his way through countless 1940 and 1950 musicals. There were politicians, military figures and even a bishop.

As for Mrs. Justin Dunning—well, she was just the woman who had spent the last eight or ten years at the great doctor's side. Jonathan didn't even know her first name. Not that it mattered.

But it did matter, he suddenly realized. And Jonathan wanted to have a name other than Mrs. Justin Dunning for her.

Fatigue and pallor could not mar the contours of her face, he thought, as he took in the pure line of her jaw, the soft fullness of her lips, the perfection with which her brows arched over her doe-brown eyes. And she was younger than Jonathan had supposed. She couldn't have been more than thirty—but then, she obviously wasn't Dunning's first wife. Dunning's teenage daughter stood at his widow's side. The present Mrs. Dunning was clearly too young to be the girl's mother. Jonathan shook the girl's hand and uttered his words of solace. "Your father was a great man. He will be missed by all of us."

The girl choked back a sob and nodded.

Then Jonathan shook hands with the senior Mrs. Dunning, an aristocratic-looking woman who stood with ramrod-straight posture. She struck Jonathan as the sort of woman who would never give in to a public display of grief. Her vivid blue eyes—so like her dead son's—stared intently into Jonathan's face.

"You are one of the residents," she said.

"Yes, ma'am. We met last month at the reception opening the new intensive care unit."

The older woman nodded, apparently satisfied with his answer, and by way of dismissal shifted her gaze to the person standing behind Jonathan in the informal queue of those wishing to offer condolences to the family.

Jonathan joined a group of residents moving away from the graveside. Their hushed conversation repeated the words Jonathan had heard so many times over the past few days.

"...such a great man."

"...struck down in his prime."

"No telling what he could have accomplished had he lived."

"I still can't believe it."

"Can't get over the irony—*him* of all people, dying of a heart attack."

And of course, such fearful mutterings as "What will happen to the Healing Arts heart program with Dunning gone?"

There were comments about the widow, too—how devoted she had been to her great husband and fragments here and there of the famous story of how Dunning had saved her life. Yes, it had been easy to make a hero out of Justin Dunning.

Jonathan got into his car and waited for those parked in front of him to leave. He sat behind the wheel, taking in the scene outside. It almost appeared to be playing in slow motion as the last of the mourners made their way past the three generations of Dunning women—mother, wife and daughter—then paused to stare one last time at the soon-to-be-buried casket, shaking their heads in a gesture of disbelief and then slowly walking through the thick carpet of grass toward their cars. Mingled with the celebrities were many people Jonathan recognized from the hospital—physicians, nurses, hospital administrators—who had worked with Dunning, some for many years. But, Jonathan wondered, who among them had really known the legendary man.

Jonathan speculated about what the younger Mrs. Dunning would do now. Would she go home to an empty house, or would there be family and friends hovering over her? Friends? Had Justin Dunning had friends? Or had there been no personal side to the man? Had he only been the public figure—the legend? Certainly he had admirers and colleagues, but somehow he seemed unapproachable on the basis of friendship. Who would have the nerve to ask one of the world's foremost heart surgeons out for a beer or for a casual game of bridge?

Surely there would be someone offering comfort to the young widow. Justin hoped so. He remembered the house filled with aunts and uncles and cousins and family friends after his father died. The neighbors, church members, tribal elders, friends of a lifetime, army buddies—they all came through the house at some time during the day of the funeral, leaving foil-wrapped offerings of food for the grieving family. Relatives had driven down from Colorado and come up from Texas. The house was filled with their suit-cases, folded-up cots and rolled-up sleeping bags for the children. The women bustled about in the kitchen, putting out the food. The men filled their plates and went out on the front steps or to the lawn chairs un-der the ancient elm tree to share their private reminis-cences of Billy Joe Sky. The young cousins played tag or catch, cautioned from time to time by the adults to keep their voices down. The oldest members of the clan sat in wicker rocking chairs on the broad front porch, talking of the old times, other deaths and other funerals, and how it seemed like only yesterday that Billy Joe Sky broke all the records at the state high school track meet or won that medal for being brave in Korea. Somehow, however, Jonathan sensed that a similar scene would not be repeated at the home of Justin Dunning.

Now that all the mourners had paid their respects to the family, the funeral director swooped forward, taking the arm of the older Mrs. Dunning, and with the widow and daughter following, escorted the women to the waiting limousine.

Jonathan turned the key in the ignition of his ancient Morgan and began to inch his way into the stream of slowly moving traffic. He drove past the limousine. The younger Mrs. Dunning was standing beside it, waiting for her mother-in-law and stepdaughter to precede her into the vehicle. She shifted her weight in a gesture that conveyed weariness. She was looking down at the ground, her shoulder sagging, her arms hanging limply. But abruptly, as though in response to an inner chastisement, she jerked her chin up and squared her shoulders. At that instant, she realized Jonathan was watching her. She met his gaze with a small nod.

The sunlight caught her hair beneath the veiled hat in such a way as to accentuate its sheen and bring out the golden highlights in its rich brown. Her eyes were the exact same color as her hair and stood out against her fair skin coloring. Her lips and cheeks were pale, devoid of any makeup. She was too fair to be without makeup in the unkind sunlight, and black was not a good color for her, yet Jonathan realized that she was lovely—not a dazzling beauty but quietly and poignantly lovely. Funny that he had never noticed before today. Now it was so obvious to him it took his breath away.

He returned her nod, then looked away. It was disturbing to be admiring the wife of the man whom he had come to bury. And he had been admiring her, Jonathan fully realized. Throughout the service at the church and during the graveside ceremony, he had watched her and had been fascinated by the naturalness with which she comforted her stepdaughter, by her innate dignity as she did her widow's duty, by the elegant way her suit draped over her body and by the beauty of her slim white neck when she tilted her head forward in prayer. Yes, he had been admiring her. Dunning's widow. He felt almost sacrilegious.

Jonathan maneuvered his car into the single lane of traffic exiting the cemetery on narrow paved lanes with names like Pleasant Vista and Journey's End on white-painted markers. Naming the streets of a cemetery struck Jonathan as rather bizarre. He supposed it helped people in locating grave sites, but he would have simply numbered them. Dr. Dunning's grave was at the intersection of Journey's End and Slumber Way. Couldn't they have come up with something less stupid? Jonathan wondered absently, his mind searching for something else to dwell on other than the hauntingly lovely face of his deceased mentor's young widow.

After all, he had never let himself get caught in the trap of mooning over any of the more appropriate women who came into his life. He wasn't about to allow the vision of Dr. Dunning's widow to distract him. When he had finished his surgical training, he would allow himself the luxury of falling in love. Not before. He was too damned poor to court a woman, and he already knew how damaging falling in love could be.

He looked in his rearview mirror. The limousine carrying the Dunning women was turning down Slumber Way, heading for the cemetery's south gate. Jonathan was committed to the stream of traffic heading north toward the hospital—toward a hospital without Justin Dunning. That was certainly going to take getting used to. Healing Arts Medical Center had been totally his creation.

He wondered about Mrs. Dunning. How difficult would it be for her to get used to living without him? What an unbelievable void must have been created in her life. Would her aloneness be unbearable?

Of course, she was young. She would grieve and then probably marry again someday.

Or would she? Other men might seem insignificant to her after being married to a legend.

Chapter One

"Dr. Sky. Paging Dr. Jonathan Sky," summoned the public address system.

Jonathan stepped to a house phone. "Sky here," he spoke brusquely.

"Dr. Sky, call Dr. Morrison," the operator instructed.

Jonathan hesitated for a minute, speculating about what business the hospital chief of staff could possibly have with him, and then he asked the operator to connect him with Dr. Morrison's office.

"Dr. Sky," the familiar, hearty voice of the chief administrative physician of the large hospital came over the phone, "my compliments on the article in the state medical journal. Very impressive. You could have been an epidemiologist if you hadn't chosen a thoracic surgery residency."

"Well, as a matter of fact, I considered it. But in the case of lung cancer, the two fields relate," Jonathan said. "Thanks for the compliment."

"You presented the material very well," Morrison continued. "Good writing style. I remember the study you did with Justin Dunning on heart disease among the state's Indian population. You wrote that up nicely, too. He was very pleased."

"Thanks," Jonathan said, wondering at this sudden interest in his reporting capabilities. "I was pleased that Dr. Dunning took an interest in my project. It was an honor to work with him."

"Sky, could you come up here for a little while," Morrison said, abruptly ending the small talk and stating the real purpose of the call. "There's someone in my office I'd like you to meet."

Jonathan checked his watch. He didn't have any time to spare. He'd have to scrub shortly to assist on a bypass operation with Dr. Ballard. Quadruple on a sixty-year-old woman who smoked and had underlying diabetes, Jonathan automatically thought.

"I won't keep you long," Morrison said, as though reading his thoughts. "Know you're busy."

"Well, it'll have to be quick, but I'll be right over," Jonathan said, relenting. After all, Morrison was the boss.

Jonathan answered another page from the intensive care unit, gave orders on a new admission and then headed for the stairs. He didn't have time to wait for an elevator.

When Jonathan entered the hospital administrator's office, the woman was standing with her back to the door, gazing out the window. Her slender form was silhouetted by the afternoon sun. Before she turned around, Jonathan knew who she was. He wasn't sure how he knew, but he did. She was Justin Dunning's widow.

Morrison was on the phone. The distinguished-looking hospital administrator waved for Jonathan to sit down.

Mrs. Dunning silently crossed the room, her footsteps muffled by the thick carpet, and took a seat on the sofa facing Morrison's desk. She was wearing a navy suit with an off-white blouse. The cut of the jacket was too severe. Clothes that were more feminine would suit her better. Her purse and a half-finished cup of coffee resided in front of her on the coffee table. She gave him a small, polite smile, then looked down at her hands in her lap, apparently electing not to begin a conversation while Morrison was on the phone.

Jonathan decided that the months since her husband's death had not been easy for her. The strain showed around her eyes. He remembered those beautiful brown eyes. Soft brown, like a doe's. He would like to see them light up in a real smile instead of one offered as a social amenity to a stranger.

She'd been spending some time in the sun, Jonathan thought. She was tanned, and her hair was sun streaked. He wondered if her tan was the result of a vacation. A cruise, maybe. To forget. Appropriate for the wealthy widow of a distinguished heart surgeon, he thought. He could have read about it on the society page, if he ever read the society page.

To avoid staring, Jonathan looked down, too. Her feet were within his field of vision. She had on navy high-heeled shoes. Simple and very expensive looking. He loved the way her arch showed over the side of the shoes. Her ankles were gorgeous. He'd never noticed ankles all that much before, but he rather enjoyed studying hers.

Morrison concluded his conversation and hastened to make introductions. "I know you're in a rush, Dr. Sky, so perhaps all I can do today is introduce you two and make arrangements for you to meet more leisurely another day. Beth, this is Dr. Jonathan Sky, the resident I was telling you about. Dr. Sky, this is Beth Dunning—Justin Dunning's widow.''

Jonathan shook hands with Beth Dunning across the coffee table without bothering to mention they had met before. He'd have to explain where.

Beth was such an old-fashioned name, Jonathan thought. Straight out of *Little Women*, whose characters he was well acquainted with, having grown up in a household with three sisters.

Jonathan had never known anyone named Beth before. He wondered how old she was and how long she had been married to Dunning. The heart surgeon had to have been a lot older than she. Jonathan recalled that he had been close to fifty at the time of his death. He guessed that Beth Dunning was closer to thirty.

The phone rang again. Morrison impatiently pushed a button on the instrument and told his secretary to hold his calls.

Morrison now directed his attention to Jonathan. "Dr. Sky, Justin Dunning left lengthy journals and a large collection of other personal papers that Mrs. Dunning is attempting to compile into a memoir suitable for publication prior to donating the material to the Justin Dunning Memorial Medical Research Library, which is to be included in our new wing. I, along with the members of the foundation board of directors, think this book would be a most fitting way to highlight the life of one of our nation's leading physicians, and it would draw attention to our heart program here at the Healing Arts Medical Center. However, not being a physician herself, Mrs. Dunning finds that she will need some help translating the technical parts of Dr. Dunning's writing into lay terms. I remember how pleased Justin was with what you wrote up on the Indian project, especially the lay version of it that appeared in a national health magazine. Justin did not hand out praise indiscriminately, and for him to allow one of his residents as much input as he allowed you must mean he was most impressed with your knowledge and ability."

"You're very kind," Jonathan said, "but Dunning knew I'd majored in English as an undergraduate and had done some writing in the past. He was a genius at discovering any sort of talent and putting it to work."

"Precisely," Morrison said. "I'd like to follow his example. It seems to me you would be the most appropriate person to work with Mrs. Dunning on this project. Literary skills and medical knowledge don't often go hand in hand. We would arrange suitable financial compensation for your time and expertise. I know you'll need to visit with Mrs. Dunning at length to find out more about the project, so we're not asking for any sort of commitment from you today. We'd just like to have you agree to talk with her about it."

Dunning's papers. Jonathan didn't have time to get involved in any project, no matter how worthy, but the prospect of dealing with his dead mentor's personal journals was tempting indeed. Jonathan had found himself propelled toward a career in cardiovascular surgery because of Dunning, although his original intention had been to complete his four-year thoracic surgery residency and return to Oklahoma. Dunning had persuaded Jonathan to apply for a two-year cardiovascular fellowship at Healing Arts when he finished his residency in thoracic surgery.

But although deeply influenced by the man's greatness, Jonathan had never been able to glean any insights into the man behind the heart surgeon. Even when they had worked briefly together on that paper, using epidemiology studies on various Southwestern Indian tribes to illustrate cultural factors in heart and lung diseases, Dunning had never let down his professional facade. Jonathan had approached Dunning about the project, knowing he himself could never get the funding needed for the project. With Justin Dunning as coresearcher, it was easy. The man had incredible connections and power, yet he was the most private person Jonathan had ever known. He kept people at a distance.

Dunning was a fascinating enigma to Jonathan, and now he was being offered an opportunity to add some pieces to the puzzle. The prospect also had enough literary merit to tempt the English major in him. And the extra money would certainly be welcome. It was at least worth looking into.

Jonathan checked his watch. He had to leave right this minute; they would be waiting for him in surgery. "Sounds fine," he said. "I don't have any free time during the day. It'll have to be in the evening or on a weekend when I'm not on call."

"How about meeting on Sunday afternoon?" Beth Dunning asked, her brown eyes questioning. "At my house?"

"Fine. About four?"

Beth nodded in agreement.

Jonathan hastily shook hands with her and Dr. Morrison, then half ran from the office.

As he raced down the well-waxed brown tiled floor of the corridor connecting the administrative wing to the surgical wing, Jonathan felt good. And he wasn't sure if it was over the prospect of working with Dunning's personal papers or of seeing his widow again. "Beth." He tested the name out loud in the empty corridor.

The name suited her. A soft, feminine, kind of sad name—or was that only because of the character in *Little Women*? That Beth was frail, and she died. Jonathan recalled his sisters crying over Beth's death no matter how many times they read that book.

If he were writing a book to go with the real-life Beth, he would keep her soft and feminine, but he certainly wouldn't have her be frail and sad. He'd have her brown eyes sparkle and her beautiful full lips laugh. He'd have her dance and sing and run barefoot in the sunshine. Her hair would trail behind her, a beautiful, unfettered mane of rich brown.

"Beth." He said her name out loud again just as he turned into the corridor leading to the surgery wing. And as he did, he almost ran into two nurses hurrying in the opposite direction in their silent, crepe-soled shoes. He could hear their giggling start as soon as they rounded the corner.

BETH WAS NERVOUS.

She finished putting on her makeup and surveyed herself in the mirror. No, too much eye shadow, she thought as she wiped some of it off.

It was almost time for Jonathan Sky to arrive, and she needed to finish dressing. She picked up a small brush and reapplied the eye shadow she had just taken off, then went to put on the blouse and slacks she had laid out on the bed.

Beth sensed that her nervousness had something to do with the fact that Jonathan Sky was a youthful and strikingly attractive man. Sky—an odd name. She wondered if perhaps he was part American Indian. He did have wonderful cheekbones that were certainly exotic-looking, if not Indian—along with intensely brown-black eyes and a lean, masculine look. Feeling a little foolish, she allowed herself to visualize him half naked astride a paint pony, surveying the prairie from atop a bluff in search of his enemies or a buffalo herd. His hair would be long and plaited, a beaded head-band spanning his forehead above dark eyes that scanned the far horizon, his bare mahogany chest painted with ancient symbols.

Beth smiled at her own fancifulness. The man's ancestor's may have played out such a scenario, but Dr. Jonathan Sky was a long way from riding ponies on the prairie. He was completing his third year of residency in one of the most prestigious thoracic programs in the country. He had to be brilliant as well as ambitious, or else he would not be where he was. Nor would he be coming to her house shortly to discuss the editing of Justin's personal papers.

Beth slipped a belt into the loops of her slacks and added a choker of pearls. She put on a gold bracelet, then took it off, deciding it seemed too frivolous.

Beth would have been far more comfortable if Martin Morrison had agreed to collaborate with her on this project himself. But when she had first approached him about the project, Martin had insisted that he was hopelessly out-of-date medically.

"I've become more of an administrator now than a physician, Beth," Martin explained. "I talked to both Christenson and Ballard about the project, but they have their own horns to toot. They are more interested in building their own reputations than in keeping the Dunning legend alive. They've lived in Justin's shadow for years, you know. Then I realized that the person to help you should be one of Justin's protégés—one of the people who trained under him. He would have a vested interest in enhancing the reputation of his mentor.''

What Martin Morrison did not say, but what Beth certainly understood, was that the Healing Arts Foundation heart program would also be enhanced by strengthening the legend of Justin Dunning. The hospital administrator had all but clapped his hands in glee when Beth suggested the memoir project.

And after he had finished gloating over the importance of saving Justin's papers and publishing them as a book, he looked at Beth fondly and said, ''You're an incredible woman, my dear. You served Justin so well in life, and now you're continuing to serve his memory. I must confess I was appalled when Justin decided to marry a woman so much younger than he was, but you were the perfect choice for him. In spite of your youth, you seemed to understand that an important man needs those around him to take care of the details of living, to free him for the work he is intended to do. In a way, our roles weren't so different. I gave up a medical practice in favor of administrative work so that this hospital and the Healing Arts Foundation would grow into a medical center worthy of Justin and his rare talent. At times, I resented it, but I knew it had to be done and that I, better than others, understood why and how. I knew how to work with Justin, how to put my own ego aside. Beth, dear, your life was like that, too. I'm sure you resented him at times but realized it would be a sin to deny true greatness. And now you serve it still with this book project.''

Beth sighed. "Yes, I served his greatness. But before you elevate me to sainthood, Martin, let me say it was probably because of my youth, and not in spite of it, that I was able to become the shadowed wife of the famous heart surgeon. And yes, I did resent it at times. Perhaps I would have taken on this book project simply because great men should be immortalized, but I'd be less than honest if I didn't admit that my primary motivation is to make money. I'm broke. Justin may have been a brilliant doctor, but he was a disaster as a businessman.''

"I knew Justin was freewheeling with his money, but I can't believe your financial situation is as extreme as you indicate,'' Morrison said, his wide brow frowning beneath a full head of carefully groomed white hair.

"Well, believe it,'' Beth said, not trying to hide the irritation in her voice. Did he think she had been lying to him? "I'm all but broke.''

Martin held up his hands in protest. "Please don't get me wrong. I'm not doubting your word. It's just that I worry about it becoming public knowledge,'' he said, his brow wrinkling in concern. "I hope you haven't told anyone else about your financial problems. It would do Justin's memory an incredible disservice.''

"Oh, I'm sure the housekeeper and gardener I had to let go understood why. And my neighbors surely have noticed that I now clean the pool myself and tend the grounds. That house is such a drain on my finances, but I can't sell it. Justin's will stipulated that the house is not to be sold but should pass on to Tricia at my death. Well, that's a lovely sentiment, but the money I was supposed to live on and run that house with just isn't there. And Justin had borrowed heavily against his life insurance. But no, I haven't spread it around that his estate consisted mostly of debts. I wouldn't intentionally tarnish his legend, Martin, if that's what you're worried about."

"Intentionally or inadvertently, we must be very careful to maintain the high regard in which Justin is held," Martin said. "It's vital to our fund-raising drive. Absolutely vital. Our future expansion here at Healing Arts could be at stake."

Martin had busied himself making lists of possible candidates for her coeditor on Justin's book but had kept referring back to the "image issue," which obviously weighed heavily on his mind. As a result, they did not come to a decision about a collaborator for the book project at that first meeting. Beth made an appointment with Martin to continue their discussion the following afternoon, after he had taken time to think about it.

Later Martin had added and discarded names to the list of potential collaborators until at last he had boiled the names down to three, with Dr. Sky being his first choice.

So here she was, Beth thought as she stared at herself in the mirror for the tenth time in the last twenty minutes, apprehensive to the point that her stomach hurt, waiting for an intense young man with a strange name and with eyes that looked as if they could see into the past century. Or maybe he wasn't so young. After all, he was a third-year resident. In addition to the three years in the residency program, he would have had four years of college and four years of medical school under his belt. That meant he was at least twenty-nine or thirty—about her age. But she felt older. Being married to an older man and becoming a mother to his child had forced her to step into the role of an older person. It was as though she had never had a youth, for poor health had robbed her of a normal early childhood and adolescence, and she had given the rest of her life to Justin. She would continue to think of Dr. Sky as younger. Somehow it made her more comfortable.

Beth finished dressing and wandered into the living room. According to the clock on the mantel, Dr. Sky was five minutes late. Of course, that shouldn't surprise her, and she quickly put aside her irritation. She understood. Physicians usually were late, if they showed up at all. Illness did not schedule itself conveniently to fit around doctors' schedules. How could you get angry if someone who was off healing a fellow human being was late for an appointment with you?

She wanted a drink but suppressed the desire. Instead, she went back to the kitchen and put on a pot of water for tea. She stood at the kitchen window, staring out into the half-acre backyard with its stately palms, view of the ocean and beautifully landscaped swimming pool. The Southern California look. The good life right off the pages of *Better Homes & Gardens*. But her husband had died in that pool. She would have liked to have the damned thing taken away, but pools were planted to stay firmly in place, demanding their ration of expensive chemicals and producing green fungus if you didn't care for them properly.

Beth took her cup of tea out onto the terrace, leaving the French doors open so that she could hear the doorbell. The view of the ocean beyond the row of palm trees was beautiful. Beth had trained herself to look past the pool and to concentrate instead on the ocean. Now that Justin was gone, she supposed she could clear away some of the palms and open up the view. She had suggested that once, but Justin had told her the mature palms were prized and one didn't go around cutting them down. But somehow palm trees never seemed like real trees to her. They didn't have leaves and branches. They looked as if they were made of rubber in a factory in Akron, Ohio, instead of growing naturally. But then she wasn't a native of Southern California and probably didn't have the proper appreciation for tropical vegetation. Most of the places she had lived during her growing-up years had less temperate climates. She had come to California to attend UCLA after going to secondary school in Switzerland. Her diplomat father lived in France with his second wife and two younger children.

Beth checked her watch again. Jonathan Sky was only thirty minutes late so far. Any more than that and he really should call or have someone call for him—unless he was operating and his appointment with her was relegated to the far reaches of his mind while he fought for a patient's life.

Déjà vu, Beth thought. Here she was waiting for a doctor again. At least there wasn't a meal waiting along with her.

When the sun touched the horizon, she acknowledged that Dr. Sky was not coming. She went in to fix dinner. Tricia would be home soon. Beth decided on omelets. They could eat in front of the television, something they had done a lot of in the past year. A year. It really had been almost a year. The anniversary of Justin's death was just two weeks away.

Instead of preparing a meal, she found herself wandering about the house again, restless. She had spent three days organizing her thoughts and Justin's papers in preparation for this evening, for Jonathan Sky's arrival. Now she had to get used to the idea that he would not be here.

She turned on lamps in the living room and rearranged the objects on the coffee table. Dinner, she reminded herself, and headed for the kitchen. She wasn't hungry, but Tricia would be.

Tricia came in the backdoor wearing shorts over her bathing suit and carrying her beach bag casually over a well-tanned shoulder. Summer had barely begun, but already she had a golden tan that made her pale blond hair all the more striking.

Beth felt her face breaking into a smile. Seeing Tricia made her feel better.

Tricia kissed Beth on the cheek. "Omelets again," she noted as she checked dinner preparations. Tricia wrinkled her nose. "I'm going to start clucking instead of talking pretty soon."

"They're filling, nutritious and cheap," Beth informed her blond stepdaughter. "Most of all cheap. We're on a tight budget, remember?"

"How could I forget?" Tricia said in a teasing voice. "You certainly remind me often enough. I'm expecting bread and water any day now. I'll go shower off the sand and come make a salad. I'm so hungry, I guess I can manage to get an omelet down, but put on lots of cheese and mushrooms."

"Bread and water? Why didn't I think of that?" Beth asked. "I don't have mushrooms, but I'll double up on the cheese."

Beth put the skillet on to heat and was checking the television schedule when the phone rang. "Mrs. Dunning, this is Nurse Gary calling from surgery," the businesslike female voice said. "Dr. Sky asked me to call and say that he regrets he cannot keep his appointment with you."

Ah, yes, déjà vu, Beth thought as she hung up. Well, she hoped the surgery went well. She wondered if Jonathan Sky would ever be as good as Justin had been. Where would he rank among the next generation of miracle makers?

Beth wondered if there was a Mrs. Jonathan Sky. Did Nurse Gary also call a wife, now scurrying around her kitchen, using aluminum foil to preserve her husband's dinner for late-night consumption. Mrs. Sky would have already fed the children, whom she would put to bed in a few hours, then spend the rest of the evening in solitary television viewing.

On impulse, Beth went to the desk in the living room and searched for the résumé on Dr. Sky that Martin Morrison had given her the other day. She found the stapled pages still in the envelope bearing the Healing Arts logo. Jonathan Emerson Sky. Born thirty years ago in Clearwater, Oklahoma. Phi Beta Kappa from Stanford. Rhodes Scholar finalist. No, he wasn't married.

Now why had she done that? Beth asked herself as she returned to her kitchen. It didn't matter to her one way or the other if Jonathan Sky was married. What difference could it possibly make if he had a wife at home, or a string of girlfriends? She certainly wasn't husband hunting. There were times when Beth honestly doubted if she would ever marry again.

Not that she didn't believe in marriage. If it worked out, she supposed it could be grand. But for her the idea of marriage was not appealing. And if she ever did marry again, she didn't think it should be to a clone of Justin Dunning. After a year away from it, Beth was beginning to realize that her marriage to the famous heart surgeon had not been a healthy one.

Chapter Two

"Mrs. Dunning, how are you?" Jonathan said, politely shaking hands with Beth.

Beth nodded, offering a perfunctory "fine" to his inquiry and quickly withdrawing her hand. "Won't you come in?"

"I'm sorry about last Sunday," Jonathan said, stepping into the entry hall. "I had to assist on one of Dr. Christenson's cases. One of his transplants was going bad. We had to do a second transplant, and you know how fast things have to move when a donor is located. The patient was a twenty-two-year-old woman. A mother, with two kids. I'm not sure how much time we bought her, though. There are signs she's rejecting this heart, too."

"I understand very well the demands on a physician's time," Beth said as she led him into the living room. "Don't worry about last Sunday."

Jonathan let out a low whistle as he stood at the top of the three steps that led down into the spacious sunken living room, with its cream-colored carpet and a windowed wall that revealed a panoramic view of the ocean. "Wow," he said. "So this is how the better half lives. It's beautiful."

Beth looked around the tastefully furnished room, trying to see it through the eyes of a poorly paid resident. Yes, it was beautiful, but it no longer touched her. She was too busy keeping up the expensive oceanside house and struggling to pay the taxes to enjoy its beauty. Even the ocean had lost its magic for her. It was too unrelenting, too awesome, too incomprehensible. It made her feel insignificant and unimportant. Sometimes she thought about living someplace else—someplace with a horizon a little closer to home, with ordinary trees in the backyard, someplace on a more human scale.

Jonathan accepted her offer of a drink and wandered over to stare out the window while Beth mixed his bourbon and water from behind the room's spacious bar. He was wearing a beige sport coat over an open-collared navy shirt. His skin was bronze, and he was slim hipped and broad shouldered, looking more like an athlete than a physician. He was even more attractive on second meeting than Beth remembered. Or was attractive the right word? His appearance was too striking and powerful for such a routine term. He was different in a very special way. Tricia would call him a "hunk," but Beth could think of no suitable word from her own vocabulary. She just knew that she would be more comfortable if he were shorter and plumper and had hazel eyes under pale brows instead of vividly dark ones under heavy, important brows.

His hair was straight and black. His face was broad and powerful. His nose would overwhelm a lesser face, but it belonged on his face, with its square, strong jaw and full mouth. And of course there were those cheekbones.

"Are you Indian?" she asked abruptly.

"Yes, I'm three-quarters Kiowa and Delaware."

"What's it like?" she asked. "Do you feel truly Indian, or is it just an interesting aside, like my being German and Scotch-Irish?"

Beth indicated that his drink was ready. She remained behind the bar to pour herself a gin and tonic. Jonathan crossed the large room. He moved very well. Maybe he was an athlete.

She pushed his drink across the bar and withdrew her hand quickly lest her fingers accidentally touch his.

He took a sip of his drink and nodded appreciatively before he answered.

"No, my being Indian is not just an interesting aside," he said. "It's much more than that. I was raised to feel my Indian heritage very deeply, and I still do—though not as much as I used to, I must admit. My folks considered themselves Indians first and other things after that. I think I consider myself first to be an American, then a physician and then maybe an Indian. When I was a kid back in Oklahoma, I decided to make a doctor of myself and practice among my people. Indians have a lot more health problems than the population at large, and I felt compelled to address these problems. And even in medical school I had a vague notion that I'd either work at an Indian hospital when I finished my residency or perhaps go into epidemiology and do research into the cause of some of those health problems. Or go into the public health field and work at preventing some of them."

"But now you'd rather follow my husband's footsteps and be a cardiovascular surgeon?" Beth asked, taking a sip of her own drink. And then another. She was nervous. She hoped it didn't show.

"Something like that," he admitted, slipping onto one of the leather-covered bar stools. "Open-heart surgery and organ transplanting aren't done in Indian hospitals. Medicine is a whole lot more basic at those institutions. I'm pretty much locked into large medical centers like Healing Arts if I go into cardiovascular surgery. Of course, no one will ever have the impact that your husband and men like Michael DeBakey and Christiaan Barnard had. They were pioneers. Giants in their fields. Now it's growing so rapidly that no one individual will have the sort of influence Dr. Dunning had. He came along at a time when he could make a maximum impact. I must admit I'm intrigued by the prospect of getting a more personal glimpse of his career through his writings."

"Well, there's lots to glimpse—what with his journals and all the letters," Beth said, launching into a little statement she had mentally prepared for Dr. Sky's benefit. "They give a very comprehensive look at his training and research and career—and the creation of the Healing Arts Foundation. It was endowed almost exclusively by some of Justin's former patients, you know. Justin was quite eloquent when he wrote about his work. Death and infirmity were his personal enemies, and he couldn't stand to lose a fight. His remarkable personality is very apparent in his writings. He was..."

Her voice trailed off. She forgot what she planned to say next. Jonathan's gaze on her face as she spoke was disconcerting. Embarrassed, she took another sip of her drink.

"It must have been very difficult this past year, losing him so suddenly," Jonathan said, his voice filled with genuine sympathy. "You must be very lonesome."

The sympathy in his voice elicited an uncustomary wave of self-pity that lodged in Beth's throat and threatened to bring tears to her eyes.

"Yes, it's been a lonely year," she said, swallowing to dissipate the feeling. It was true. Justin's death had left a huge, gaping void. It had taken away the center around which her life turned. It had robbed her of financial security and even of her very identity. Like debris caught up in the vortex of a tornado that suddenly stilled, Beth and her stepdaughter had dropped to the ground, disoriented and frightened by the sudden quiet.

"Well, I guess you're anxious to have a look at the journals," Beth remarked, unable to think of anything else to say to Jonathan Sky. Again she wished that Martin Morrison had agreed to help her with this editing. This man, with his intense, dark gaze and lean, powerful build was disconcerting. She found herself wanting to stare at him, yet she was almost too embarrassed to meet his eyes when he spoke to her.

"Bring your drink," Beth said, picking up her own and coming out from behind the bar. "I've laid out the papers in Justin's study. You might as well get acquainted with them."

As she led the way down the hallway, she could feel him looking at the V of her bare back above her summery dress. It felt as if her back were blushing.

Beth had set up card tables in the study and organized the papers by years. She could tell that Jonathan was not prepared for the amount of material she had assembled. It was going to be quite an editing project.

Now he will say he doesn't have time for a project like this, Beth thought. And she wouldn't blame him. Time was the one thing a resident physician had the least of.

"Of course, you'd receive a percentage of the book's proceeds when it's published," Beth hastened to tell him. "And I understand Dr. Morrison will arrange for the foundation to pay you an honorarium in advance if you take on the project."

There were two other names on Martin's list of potential editors, Beth reminded herself. If Jonathan declined, they would just have to ask someone else. She almost hoped that would be the case. She wasn't sure she could be comfortable working with this man. He was nice enough and certainly polite. But his very masculine presence in her home was disquieting.

She found herself holding her breath as he surveyed the stacks of material.

"How much of this have you read?" Jonathan asked.

"All of it," Beth replied. "I've marked the parts that I think should be published and indicated what needs editing by someone with medical expertise. Some of it's written so technically, it would be impossible for the layman to read. I don't understand it well enough myself to put it into simple terms. I'm sure Justin wrote a lot of it with publication as a goal, but I think perhaps he had a more professional audience in mind than the mass-market book I envision."

Jonathan went first to the stack of leather-bound journals. There were ten in all, handwritten, covering the past twenty-three years of Justin's life. A smaller, sixth book had his reminiscences of his childhood, youth and lengthy medical training.

Jonathan picked up one of the journals and seated himself in Justin's chair. Beth took a seat on the sofa and watched as the handsome physician lost himself in her husband's words.

How strange it was to see another man sitting in Justin's chair, Beth mused. She was sure Jonathan would not have seated himself there if he had realized how firmly in her mind that chair was associated with her dead husband. But of course he had no way of knowing.

Jonathan Sky did not look as stern as Justin used to appear. Justin always sat straight and tall, his head centered between the two wings on the chair back. But there was a relaxed easiness about the way Jonathan stretched his long legs out in front of him and leaned one elbow on the armrest. He looked approachable. She would not have hesitated to interrupt him.

The young resident was obviously captivated as the portrait of Justin Dunning revealed itself on the handwritten pages. He turned page after page, never looking up, reading with a discernible intensity. Beth wondered if he had forgotten she was in the room with him.

She closed her eyes to visualize what he was seeing—Justin's precise, legible script, so uncharacteristic of a physician, spelling out case after case of people who should have died but did not because their surgeon dared to open their heart to mend the havoc wrought by age or abuse or illness.

She picked up one of the journals herself, absently looking over words with which she was already familiar.

There was a slight breeze coming from the door that opened on to the patio. She closed the journal and allowed it to slide from her lap. It was easier to concentrate on the breeze with her eyes closed. It felt good on her bare arms.

IT WAS TWILIGHT when she opened her eyes again. She was on her side, her body curled into a comfortable curve, her head on a throw pillow. Jonathan was kneeling beside the sofa, shaking her gently.

"Mrs. Dunning," he said softly, "I'm going now."

The feel of his fingers on her bare arm was interesting, Beth thought groggily as she struggled her way to consciousness. It felt particularly nice, his touch. How strange. Really nice. It was as though tiny magnets in her skin were responding to matching magnets in his. Infinitesimal magnetic currents teased the sensors just under her skin, pleasuring them in a most extraordinary way. She tried to remember if she had ever experienced a similar feeling.

But before she could make this determination, he withdrew his touch. The abrupt end to the pleasant sensation pushed Beth the rest of the way across the threshold between sleep and wakefulness.

Beth realized she had been asleep.

Asleep!

She couldn't believe she had done anything so humiliating. Mortified, she pulled her skirt down over a partially exposed thigh and struggled into a sitting position.

"I'm so embarrassed," Beth said. "I guess I dozed off a bit."

"No problem," Jonathan said kindly. He was still kneeling beside the sofa. His face was almost level with hers, and very close. Such a decidedly masculine face. That jaw. The nose. Those cheekbones. The

heavy brows. The deep cleft in his chin. The firm outline of his full mouth. It was intimidating to have such
a face so near to hers.

"You looked so peaceful lying there," he was saying. "It was rather a special treat for me, sharing a
room with a beautiful sleeping woman."

Beth's hand went to her throat. She could feel the
flush mounting there. She didn't know whether to feel
embarrassed over the sexual overtones of his words or
to feel flattered by his saying she was beautiful. But
then he probably didn't really mean either. He was just
being charming. It came naturally to him. She thought
Indians were supposed to be stoic and nonverbal. Apparently Jonathan Sky didn't know about the stereo-
type.

Feeling totally flustered, Beth did not respond to his
comment. Instead, she asked, "Did you have a chance
to read much? Do you have any questions?"

"Hundreds. And yes, I read quite a bit. Fascinating material. Your husband certainly manufactured his
own destiny. He reminds me of an evangelist; only instead of selling religion, he was selling health. 'Give
me your trust and your money, and I'll give you a
miracle.' I had no idea he actually sought out wealthy
people with heart conditions and convinced them to let
him mend their valves and bypass their clogged arteries and replace their worn parts. God, it was so
unethical. Solicitation. Physicians just don't do that,
but look at what he accomplished. He built one of the
finest private research facilities in the country for cardiovascular research. He was one of the first to prove
that such facilities could be financed through the private sector. He dared. And for him it paid off. I think
this will make quite a book, Mrs. Dunning."

"Please call me Beth," she said, suddenly hating the formality of "Mrs. Dunning" and wondering why she had not thought to tell him to use her first name sooner. So few people called her by her first name since her marriage to Justin. Even people she would invite to use it often ignored her request. After all, they apparently reasoned, they didn't call her husband by his first name.

But Jonathan Sky nodded his head in acquiescence. "Beth," he said in acknowledgment. The sound of her name on his lips pleased her. It made her feel more like his contemporary—something she now wanted.

"Then does that mean you'll help me get this into some sort of readable form?" she asked, suddenly hopeful. She wanted him to say yes. She wanted it very much.

"I'll give you what time I have," Jonathan said. "The prospect of extra money is attractive. As you probably know, resident physicians receive very small salaries. And I think the project is definitely worthwhile, but the pace may be slow. My life is controlled by the almighty clock. Which reminds me, I'd better get on back to the hospital. I still have some preoperative physicals to work up tonight."

"Could I fix you some coffee first? Or a sandwich? My daughter made some cookies." Beth realized she wasn't just being polite. A mental image of the two of them enjoying coffee on the patio flashed across her mind. Moonlight on the ocean. Soft music coming from the outside speakers.

"No, thanks. I have to get back. May I take a couple of these journals with me? Perhaps I can read them between patients, when I have emergency room duty."

She walked with him to his car. They decided on Wednesday and Sunday afternoons for a work schedule—unless he was on call, of course. Or there was an emergency. How familiar this all seemed, Beth thought. She remembered all of the times during her marriage that plans were left up in the air, but she pushed the thought from her mind. "I'll have a snack for us next Wednesday," Beth said, surprised at how eager her voice sounded.

"That'll be great," Jonathan said. They were standing beside his funny little sports car now. Could he really fit his tall frame into that small a car?

There was no reason for him not to get into the car and drive away, but still Jonathan stood there looking down at her. The last rays of the sun set his face in a glowing relief, the right side illuminated by the golden light, the left side in shadows.

But her face was also bathed in the golden light, she realized when he said softly, "Right now I wish I were an artist instead of a physician. You are so beautiful, and the light on your face is incredible. It should be captured on canvas."

He'd called her beautiful again. How could he say that? Beth knew how she looked—not unattractive but certainly not beautiful. She looked up at him. His look was so frankly admiring, it took her breath away.

"I remember you at the funeral," Jonathan said suddenly. "That must have been rough—all those people telling you how stunned they felt about his death when you were the one most directly affected. I would have liked to have done something for you, but nothing seemed appropriate. Back home I could have offered to chop your firewood for the winter or hoe your vegetable garden in the spring. And my mother's quilting club would have brought in food. But life is simpler in Clearwater, Oklahoma.''

"We're both a very long way from places like Clearwater," Beth said, but she was touched. She almost wished that were not the case and that he had come to chop firewood for the Widow Dunning. He would be in the backyard of her mythical Clearwater home, his shirt off, lifting the ax time and again, clean-smelling wood chips flying in wild disarray around him. There would be sweat covering his muscular torso as he cut and stacked her a winter's worth of firewood. And would she be bustling about the kitchen, making some suitable home-cooked delicacy to reward his efforts?

Ah, such fanciful ideas, Beth thought, forcing her mind into a more realistic vein. They were in San Diego, not Clearwater, Oklahoma. There was a fireplace in her house—a huge stone one whose chimney soared upward to the living room's cathedral ceiling. But the few times a year she lit a fire, it was composed of artificial logs purchased at the supermarket.

And a young surgeon aspiring for a world-class career didn't chop wood in the backyard of an elegant oceanside home in San Diego's fashionable La Jolla area. He might injure his hands. The neighbors might see a man wielding an ax and call the police. And what would he chop? The palm trees?

"Until Wednesday," he said, and extended his hand.

But it was more intimate than a handshake. Their hands lingered within each others. Beth stared at the merged hands—hers smaller, lighter toned. His fingernails were clipped very short, just as Justin had worn his. His fingers were longer than Justin's but more slender. And where Justin had a covering of dark hair over the back of his hands, Jonathan's were smooth.

But even more interesting than the way his hand looked was the way it felt. Jonathan's hand was magic. It was cool to the touch yet somehow transferred warmth into her flesh—warmth that radiated up her arm. Her response to his touch confused her.

"Maybe I shouldn't tell you this," Jonathan said, "but I've thought about you a lot over the past year."

He was still holding her hand. He thought she was special. He liked the way she looked. Beth wasn't used to compliments or hand holding. She didn't know what she should do next. A wave of embarrassment brought a flush to her cheeks. She felt foolish. What if he noticed that she was blushing? She slipped her fingers from his grasp and spoke in a brusque tone that implied dismissal, even though she wasn't sure she wanted him to leave. She did not know how else to handle the situation.

"I appreciate your help," she said. "Good evening."

Jonathan nodded and quickly folded himself into the tiny car. He waved out the open window as he drove away, his tires spinning on the loose gravel of the drive.

He should have kept his mouth shut, Jonathan thought with chagrin as he turned on to La Jolla Boulevard. Now he'd embarrassed and upset her. What in the world possessed him to admit he had been thinking about her since her husband's funeral? She probably misunderstood altogether what he was trying to say. It wasn't as though he'd been thinking about calling her up and asking her out. But Jonathan had been impressed with her dignity at the funeral. And he had carried a memory of her in his mind's eye. He could see her still, the sunlight on her hair, her sad brown eyes tinged with weariness, the smooth white of her throat above her dark suit.

Well, he'd be more careful next time, Jonathan vowed. He'd keep the conversation strictly business. If he didn't, he feared she would terminate their arrangement. And he didn't want that to happen. In fact, it was going to be very difficult to wait until Wednesday to see her again.

BETH WATCHED until the blue sports car disappeared from her driveway. The instant it was gone from her view, she turned and raced back into the house, ran down the hall and burst into her bedroom where she stood breathless in front of the mirror over her dressing table.

She studied the image of the woman in the mirror. Was she or was she not beautiful? Could it possibly be some sort of distortion in his vision? For whatever reason, Beth desperately wanted to believe that at least to this man she was indeed beautiful.

She reached up to unpin her hair and allow it to fall over her shoulders. She reached for the blusher and added more color to her pale cheeks. She touched up her lipstick. Then she picked up a hand mirror and studied her face from all angles. She added more eye shadow and studied herself again. She changed her earrings and looked again. She just wasn't sure.

Beth removed the earrings and dropped them back into her jewelry box. Restlessly, she wandered around the room. The pictures hanging over the bed needed straightening. That took her about fifteen seconds.

She closed the draperies and then reopened them again. She rearranged the objects on her bedside table and found herself staring at the picture of her dead husband that resided there. She tried to remember if Justin had ever called her beautiful. Usually, if he said anything at all about her appearance, it was a simple "You look very nice, my dear."

She went out into the kitchen to search for something to eat. Tricia was in Oceanside, visiting her grandmother, so Beth had not yet considered dinner. But she really didn't feel hungry, just restless. She opened the refrigerator for a while and stared at the food inside. A salad. She could fix a salad. But she grabbed a stalk of celery instead, and wandered out by the pool. She switched on the lights, the underwater pool light immediately turning the pool into a vivid gem—a gigantic glowing aquarium.

The water looked inviting. Beth kept the pool immaculate, but she hadn't been in it since Justin's death. She used to swim a lot, laps mostly, back and forth fifty or sixty times until exhaustion overtook her.

Filled with undirected energy, she walked around the pool, crunching on her celery. If it weren't dark, she would have gone jogging on the beach, but she had better sense than to go down there by herself after dark. At the end of the second turn around the pool, she stopped off at the kitchen for a glass of Chablis. She forced herself to sit in a chaise lounge and to sip slowly.

The wine relaxed her a little. But she still had a tremendous urge to do something physical. She got up, thinking she might go clean cupboards or mop a floor. But the ripples in the water had a seductive effect on her. She remembered the cool feel of the water lapping against her wet skin.

But she hadn't been in the pool for a very long time. It had reached the point where she thought she would never use it again. The pool was tainted. Justin had not drowned in its waters, but he had had a heart attack and died there. Swimming in the pool seemed inappropriate now. In fact, the pool's presence in her backyard had become an obscenity to Beth.

Tonight, however, it didn't look obscene, only inviting. After all, the pool hadn't killed Justin, Beth found herself rationalizing. A heart attack had. A coronary occlusion to be more exact. He just happened to be in the pool when it occurred. He could have been in his car, or even in the operating room. But after a year of feeling repelled by the pool, why was she having this change of attitude tonight?

Just because time has a way of putting things right, Beth told herself. It had nothing to do with the attention paid to her by a young physician with the unusual name. Sky. Jonathan Sky. Beth looked up at the sky. A half moon and ten million stars glorified the heavens. She got up and switched off the yard lights to see the stars more clearly. There, that was better. Now there were twenty million. She could stretch out on the chaise and study them.

But instead of returning to the lounge chair, she undid the ties on her sundress and let it drop to the deck. She slipped out of her sandals and underwear. She marveled that she was doing such a thing. Never in her life had she undressed anyplace except behind a closed door. And it would seem she was about to go skinny-dipping. Not only had she never swum naked in this or any other swimming pool, it had never occurred to her to do so.

Beth did not test the water first. Without hesitating, she went straight to the diving board and took three measured steps, gave a small spring and arched her naked body over the moon-kissed water. The initial cold as she plunged into it was shocking—totally so. She kicked her way to the surface and erupted from the water's depths with a war hoop. She had forgotten what a shock diving into untested water could be. But God, it was invigorating!

She hadn't realized that swimming in the nude felt different from swimming in a suit. But it did. There was no fabric, no prudery, nothing between her and the water. She felt so unfettered, so free. And something else. Sensual? Naughty? She wasn't sure. She just knew it was something new.

And it wasn't only the absence of a suit that caused this feeling of being at one with the water, of being free. The shock of the cold water seemed to have relaxed something within her mind. Maybe it was like a mental patient having electric shock therapy. Well, she had experienced a new shock therapy of her own, Beth decided. And she felt changed because of it.

For almost a year, sadness and worry and guilt had been her constant companions. But here in this cold, pure water, she was finally free of them.

She plunged back under the water, going to the bottom of the pool and, with bent knees, pushing off from it to propel herself to the surface. She arched her body out of the water and plunged back again and again like a frolicking porpoise. In and out. In and out.

She felt so alive, as if she had been cut free after being bandaged under so many layers of gauze that all sensation was lost. Now the bandages had been removed, and her skin rejoiced. Hallelujah, her skin seemed to say. How wonderful to feel again!

Beth's body and mind were caught up in the pure sensation, with all conscious thought being pushed aside. She was at one with the water. Elemental water. Purifying water. She was a fish. A mermaid. She was quicksilver moonlight skimming its surface.

It felt good. Damned good. Glorious.

But later, when exhaustion had finally brought her antics to an end, the exaltation began to leave her. She swam to the shallow end and climbed up the steps, then hastened to grab her sundress and hold it over her nakedness. No one was there to see her, but suddenly she felt ashamed.

She went to her bathroom and showered away the chill with piercing streams of hot water, then, wrapped in a terry robe, sat down in front of the vanity mirror and stared at her reflection. Except for a dazed look about the eyes, her face still appeared basically the same, but the person who had been swimming naked shortly before was someone with whom Beth had no acquaintance.

What the hell had happened to her out there? Where had all those feelings come from? They hadn't completely gone away even yet, she realized as she trailed her fingers across her cheek, down her throat and over her breasts. She still tingled with self-discovery. It was as though she had just discovered the ability of her own skin to respond to stimuli—to an admiring man's touch, to the erotic feel of cold water against her bare flesh.

Was all that because Jonathan Sky had touched her and said she was beautiful? But that could not be. A woman who would respond to a man's attentions by going crazy was an alien creature to Beth. A woman who could respond like that was a sensual creature.

Beth had never done anything crazy in her life. And at age thirty she had long ago come to the realization that she was not a sensual person. Either something in her makeup had been left out, or its potential had long since been driven away.

Until tonight, the thought of a man touching her skin was not an exciting one. In fact, she had all but decided that it would be best if she went through the rest of her life untouched.

Chapter Three

The following morning, Beth swam twenty laps in the pool. She was certainly out of shape. Fifty laps used to be her daily ritual. After her heart surgery, she had discovered the joys of a fit body and used swimming in the backyard pool as a means of exercise.

After a year's hiatus, it was nice to be swimming again. As long as she was still living in the house, she might as well use the pool, now that she had taken the initial plunge.

She sank back into the chaise lounge and stared at the half-full wineglass from last night still sitting on the chair's wooden arm. She leaned back in the chair and covered her eyes against the morning sun with her arms.

Last night. Beth pondered the phenomenon of last night as her damp body seemed to float toward the sun's warming rays. She could actually feel her skin embracing its warmth. The celebration of her own body that began last night had not yet receded. She was still so very aware of her own skin—the chill bumps, the droplets of water, the penetrating warmth of the sun's rays. Something mysterious had happened to her last night. She couldn't come down off the high yet. No adolescent girl had ever been more thrilled by the attention of the senior-class heartthrob than Beth had been by the admiring words of Jonathan Sky. She could not understand her own reaction. Not that Jonathan wasn't attractive. Goodness no! He was beautiful. And masculine. And with his Indian heritage, tantalizingly exotic. An Indian brave. The image tickled her fancy. But lots of other men were good-looking and exotic. This was California. Beautiful, exotic people were everywhere. And it wasn't as if she had never had a compliment before from a handsome man.

But Jonathan was different. His words had been more than casual compliments. He looked at her as if she were special—she herself. And that was something Beth was totally unaccustomed to. In her marriage to Justin, he had been the special one. People deferred to her and treated her well only because of her husband.

During the last years of her marriage, she had begun to resent this sort of attitude and had longed for friends who didn't even know who her husband was, or at least didn't care. She wanted something in her life that had not come to her because of the man she was married to. Perhaps she would not feel this way if her husband's fame and larger-than-life persona did not so completely overwhelm her. She wondered if she should go back to college and earn a degree. It would be nice to lose herself on a college campus, and she had even gone so far as to get catalogs from San Diego State. But Dunning was an unusual name. Someone would eventually ask. Was she related to the great heart surgeon? Then she wouldn't be anonymous anymore. People would be fascinated. They would want to know what it was like being married to such a famous man. She would have returned to being Justin's shadow.

And when she looked at the university catalog, nothing jumped out and said, "Here, study me." Many subjects interested her, but she felt that she should formulate goals. Maybe she wouldn't feel so overwhelmed by Justin's memory if she had a career of her own.

Or if she had other children. Her stepdaughter was the most fulfilling part of her life, but Tricia was growing up. And Justin hadn't wanted any more children. He had had a vasectomy during his first marriage—right after Tricia was born. And he would not discuss adoption.

But now that Justin was dead, she was having a difficult enough time managing to keep herself and Tricia afloat financially. She supposed it was just as well she didn't have the future of small children to worry about. In spite of Martin's pleas to the contrary, she was going to have to rent the house soon in order to pay some of Justin's loans that were coming due. That meant storing all of Justin's memorabilia. And that brought her thoughts back to Jonathan Sky.

Wednesday evening, the day after tomorrow, he would be here again. The thought made her nervous and apprehensive, and excited. Nothing in her previous experience could help her with these feelings. She had had crushes as a teenager—the one she remembered most clearly was a young Frenchman who worked for her father during their Paris years. Whenever she came home during school vacations, she looked forward to the times when she could visit the embassy and see Philip.

On her sixteenth birthday, he came by the apartment and brought her a bouquet of flowers.

"The face of sweet innocence," Philip said as he took her face in his hands and solemnly kissed her full on the mouth. Then he looked into her eyes and kissed her again, more deeply this time, his tongue bold and provocative.

Beth was stunned. When they all went out to dinner, she scarcely said a word the entire evening.

If Philip had any inkling of the effect his kiss had on her, his animated conversation with her father about the European Common Market and the upcoming parliamentary election did not betray it.

The next time Philip came to their house, it was to talk with her father of New York. Philip was being transferred—to work for the French delegation at the United Nations. Beth never saw him again.

Philip's two kisses were still the most memorable ones of her life. No one else had ever kissed her except Justin and his kisses were usually of the perfunctory sort.

During the years of her marriage, she had developed an aversion to her own sensuality. What few such feelings had not been eroded away by an unsatisfactory sexual adjustment in her marriage, she had consciously suppressed.

But now she felt incredibly like a teenager again. She smilingly remembered Philip. What would he think if he knew that the silly American girl thought of him after all this time? He probably didn't even remember her name, if indeed he remembered her at all. But Jonathan Sky knew who she was. And although his entrée into her life had come about because she was Justin's widow, whom she had been married to had nothing to do with his behavior toward her Sunday night. In fact, she suspected that his intent had been completely the opposite—that he hadn't planned to be anything except properly respectful to his dead mentor's wife.

So what now, Beth? she asked herself as she closed her eyes and felt her skin absorbing the rays of the morning sun. *Do you want to get involved with a clone of Justin?* Of course, it was ridiculously premature even to be thinking such things, but what if she fell in love with Jonathan and he with her? What if they married? Or did she want at least to try being her own person, whoever that was. She didn't know what she was capable of, what her talents and limits were, what potential, if any, she had. If only Jonathan were a more ordinary person, she could dream of marrying him and having a family to raise. What if he were a shopkeeper and they could work together in a family business? But he wasn't ordinary. He wasn't a shopkeeper. And shouldn't she be wary of rushing into another relationship, especially one as potentially stifling as with another heart surgeon?

The answer was, of course, yes. Intellectually, Beth knew this as surely as she knew night would follow day. But the rest of her refused to compute this information. Her whole body fairly glowed with the thought of seeing Jonathan Sky again. She couldn't remember the last time she had felt such a sense of anticipation.

Well, Jonathan was going to come on Wednesday regardless, she decided with a sigh as she rose and slipped into her robe. So she might as well enjoy planning their meal, deciding what to wear and wondering if he would touch her again. Yes, she was definitely going to enjoy preparing for Wednesday night.

"You're sick, Beth Dunning," she muttered out loud as she hurried down the hall toward Tricia's room.

"Talking to yourself is the first sign of senility," Tricia said as she appeared in the doorway of her room, hairbrush in hand. Her tan legs contrasted with her white shorts, and her blond hair was complemented by her turquoise-colored shirt. Sometimes when Beth looked at her daughter, she couldn't believe this lovely girl on the brink of womanhood was the same skinny, frightened little girl who stole her heart ten years ago. Tricia was now shapely and almost as tall as Beth. But then Beth would look again, and she would see the same dimpled smile, the same sweet expression, the same vulnerable look in those blue eyes that Tricia had as a child.

"So I hear," Beth said. "Do you have time to breakfast on the terrace? I thought I'd do some French toast."

"Sounds fantastic. Does this red belt look okay with this skirt, or should I go for black?"

"Red, definitely," Beth said.

"I heard you out in the pool," Tricia said, her blue eyes solemn.

"Does that bother you?" Beth asked. "If it does, I won't swim anymore."

"I'm not sure," Tricia replied, her tone uncertain. "I know how much you liked to swim, and I know it shouldn't bother me. It's just an inanimate pool."

"But your father died there," Beth said, hugging Tricia to her. "And you have every right in the world to feel strange about it. What would you think of renting this house with its pool and unpleasant memories about your dad's death? We could move into someplace smaller.''

"Move?'' Tricia asked, pulling away from Beth and staring at her, a look of fear creeping into her eyes. "From this house? Oh, Beth, I love this house. It's the only home I've ever known. It's all I have left of my parents. I can feel my mother here. And Daddy. It's where we were a family. It's where you and Daddy and I were a family. Can't you and I stay here and keep on being a family?''

"We'll try, honey," Beth said. "But it takes so much money to keep up a house like this.''

"I always thought Daddy had lots of money. What about his investments? Can't we sell something? I know he would have wanted you to spend his money keeping this house for us. He wouldn't want his wife and daughter to live anyplace else.''

Anyplace else, Beth thought as she headed for the kitchen, meaning someplace common and ordinary, like where the rest of the world lived. Yes, Tricia was right. Justin would have been horrified to think that his wife and daughter might one day have to live in an ordinary house or apartment. That would reflect badly on him. But if Justin had wanted them to live well, he should have made some provisions for it. He built this grand house and never paid for it. He borrowed heavily against his life insurance. He didn't start trust funds or savings accounts. Instead, he poured most of his money back into his foundation, his monument to himself.

Of course, he did accomplish so much. Justin was a genius. But geniuses are sometimes not fully developed human beings. They suffer from tunnel vision and are able to see only one small segment of the human condition.

But why did she not have this wisdom before—before it was too late to effect a change in her and Justin's lives? Suddenly, more than ever before, Beth wished Justin were alive again and standing right beside her in the kitchen. She would have given anything to have him back with her. Maybe, just maybe, if she had the chance, she could have made him understand that there's more to life than one's profession, no matter how noble that profession may be. Maybe she could have helped him experience life more fully. Maybe she could have enticed him to beat the eggs while she set the table. There had been no shared little things like that in their life. And if she could have taken the blinders off Justin and forced him to look objectively at his life and their marriage, if she had at least tried to do that, she might have found the courage to take control of her own life. It seemed so cruel and incredibly unfair that it took Justin's death to give her another chance with life. She would have much preferred for it to come out of her own decision making and not out of tragedy. The tragedy of death tainted her freedom to start over again.

But tainted or not she had it now. Freedom. What was she going to do with it? She could continue to serve her husband even after his death, somehow finding a way to maintain this ostentatious house as a tribute to him, somehow pretending he had provided well for his family when in fact he had not. Or she could try to begin to make a new life for herself.

And what if the new life turned out to be a repeat of the old one? A life dedicated to serving a husband's greatness and living in his shadow?

"Damn you, Jonathan Sky," she said into the wall mirror that hung over the buffet in her spacious dining room.

Why did the first man to ever make her feel like a complete woman have to be another heart surgeon in the making? She didn't want someone who could walk on water. How normal it would seem to be able to get irritated with one's husband because he was late coming home or didn't show up for dinner and not have to be forever understanding because, after all, he was saving another human being's life. How wonderful it would be to have a husband who had time for a family. It would be easier to deal with a flesh-and-blood mistress than the mistress who had always controlled Justin's life and now would be in control of Jonathan Sky's.

Beth tied an apron around her middle and stared at the kitchen counter, trying to remember what she was supposed to be doing. Breakfast. She went to the refrigerator and got out the milk and eggs. The bread was in the bread box on top of the refrigerator. She took out a bowl and a fork.

Beth sprinkled cinnamon on the eggs and one by one dipped the slices of bread in the mixture and placed them on the grill.

"I'm sorry, Justin," she whispered.

She was sorry that she hadn't grown up sooner. There had been so many unsolved issues in their marriage, and they didn't even know it. They weren't very good for each other. She enabled him to be domineering and arrogant because of her immaturity and weakness. But Beth was wiser now. If Justin were still alive, they would at least have the opportunity to discuss their differences.

"I'm truly sorry," she said again, and wiped a tear from her eye with the back of her hand.

WHEN, JONATHAN RETURNED to the hospital after leaving Beth's house, all hell had broken loose. He had forgotten that he had promised one of his fellow residents earlier in the week that he would cover for him Sunday evening. The resident had checked out to him, but Jonathan had not taken a pager with him to Beth's house or told the hospital operator where to locate him in case of emergency, something he routinely did even if he wasn't on call. And there *had* been an emergency. Two of them, as a matter of fact. Surgery was in progress on one of Dr. Christenson's transplants who had started hemorrhaging from an aortic-valve replacement. And earlier in the evening a triple bypass of Dr. Ballard's had failed and a second operation had to be scheduled.

Christenson was furious.

"So this is the sort of professionalism we can expect to see in one of Dunning's handpicked protégés," he hissed, ripping off his surgical mask. "I guess you know, Doctor, that this is inexcusable. Surgery on the patient had to be delayed for over an hour while we located someone else to assist."

Christenson had every right to be furious, Jonathan conceded to himself. His behavior had been inexcusable. And he knew that Christenson could be counted on to use the incident against him in the future. Christenson was eager to damage Jonathan in any way he could—to pay him back for something that had happened just months before Dunning died. The cardiovascular surgeon had staggered into surgery one day, and Jonathan told Christenson that he was too drunk to operate. Christenson raged and raised such an uproar over Jonathan's "impertinence" that he attracted the attention of Dr. Dunning, who had been finishing up a surgery in the adjoining suite.

Dunning strolled into the operating room and quickly assessed the situation.

"Go home, Christenson," he said in a voice that was meant to be obeyed. Then the head surgeon performed the surgery himself, with Jonathan assisting.

Nothing was ever said about the incident, but Christenson had taken great pains in the year since Dunning's death to make life difficult for Jonathan.

And now the tables were turned. It had been Jonathan who had been incompetent. Christenson followed him down the hall, berating him.

"Just because you were handpicked by Dunning to be the crown prince doesn't mean a thing now," he said in a voice dripping with malice. A pair of surprised interns stepped aside to let them pass.

It was after midnight when Jonathan finally was able to go home to his small apartment. Exhausted he fell across his bed, still wearing his white hospital jacket, but he knew he wouldn't be able to sleep. He was still too angry with himself. He remembered very distinctly now telling Ron Williams that he would cover for him on Sunday night. But in all his anticipation over the upcoming visit with Beth, he completely forgot to pass the responsibility on to someone else, or at least to make sure the switchboard knew where he was. He had been too busy fantasizing about an uninterrupted evening with the personal papers and the widow of his idol.

Lately, Christenson had made it more than apparent at the hospital that the Dunning era was over as far as he was concerned, and he seemed to enjoy making things difficult for the staff physicians who had been singled out as Dunning favorites.

Jonathan vowed that nothing like this incident would ever happen to him again. He had too many years of his life invested in his medical career to let it go bad at this late date. He had always been single-minded of purpose before, able to keep out of any social entanglements that might jeopardize his future or his precarious financial standing. And he had threatened both in one weekend. On Saturday he had bought a new sport coat he could ill afford to replace the seedy one he'd been wearing since his sophomore year in college and all because he wanted to impress a woman. And then he'd become so excited over the prospect of seeing her that he'd been irresponsible and damaged his good standing in the residency program.

And he had been excited over seeing Beth again. No denying that. He was absolutely enchanted by her. Images of her had been haunting him since he met her in Dr. Morrison's office—and in a way even before that. He had to admit, there had been times during the past year when he thought about asking her out, although he was a resident with scarcely a dime to his name and three years from completing his training. He had even looked up her telephone number on one occasion.

But he realized such thoughts were pure fantasy, and he had made every effort not to dwell on them. He was years away from having any money, and he had no guarantee he would even complete his training successfully. The Healing Arts residency program—like many other highly competitive residency programs—

had a pyramid design, with far more resident physicians accepted in the first years of the program than would be allowed to complete it. Each year only the very best were asked to return, causing the others to join less prestigious programs elsewhere or to change their career goals and enter a general medical practice. Only two residents were taken into the prestigious cardiovascular program at the end of four years of thoracic residency.

Even if he had survived his specialty training and were in practice with plenty of money to devote to courtship purposes, Beth was Dunning's widow. The notion of dating her seemed totally preposterous and inappropriate. What would a woman who had been married to someone so famous think if a nobody like him asked her out? She'd either be amused or angry.

And even if she hadn't been married to a world-class heart surgeon, why would a woman who lived in a house like hers and who was accustomed to every nicety that life had to offer want to go out with a penniless resident who grew up in a small frame house in a rural Oklahoma town. Jonathan still felt out of place in elegant surroundings and wondered if he always would. He didn't know about wines and symphonies. He had never had the opportunity to polish off the rough edges of his simple upbringing.

But now the distance that separated them seemed a little more bridgeable. She was not only beautiful, but he had discovered that she was a warm, approachable human being. Last Sunday he had practically had to sit on his hands to keep from touching her.

For a minute there he actually was considering kissing her soft, full lips.

Jonathan groaned out loud in his tiny bedroom at the thought. A wave of yearning washed over him. He wanted that very much. His mouth covering hers, kissing her deeply. His arms would be around her, pulling her body tight against him. He thought of his hands on her back and in her hair. He opened his hands and held them in front of his face. Those hands—the places he had wanted to put them.

You're getting on dangerous ground, old boy, he warned himself. He had three more years of training to complete, he reminded himself again. He was a poor Indian boy from Oklahoma who had a chance to make something of himself, to break the mold of generations of stagnation.

Don't do this to yourself, he thought. *Didn't you learn your lesson after Linney?* He had almost thrown it all away during his second year of medical school because of a woman. He had come within an inch of turning his back on his medical ambition and going back to a lackluster existence as a farmer or a storekeeper in a dried-up Oklahoma town. He had almost gone back after all those years of promising himself he was going to escape, that he wasn't going to be one of those pitiful old men whittling on sticks in the town square, talking about the old days and the old ways, men who depended on the Bureau of Indian Affairs to feed them and doctor them and bury them when they died. No way. He wasn't going to end up like that. He was going to prove to young Indians that Indians could succeed despite their beginnings.

Jonathan thought of the white people in Clearwater to whom his people were considered just a bunch of "dirty-ole-Indians"—said as though it were all one word. Of course, not all of Clearwater's white population was so bigoted. Most were simply indifferent, too caught up in their own problems to care about those of the Indians. And some white people in Clearwater regarded the Indians simply as citizens of the town who happened to be Indian. But the vocal minority had tainted his childhood and that of every other Indian child who grew up in such towns.

Jonathan had always known he had a lot to prove. His father, Billy Joe Sky, had become a self-fulfilling prophecy for those "fine" Clearwater citizens. Billy Joe had never amounted to anything, he drank too much, did cheap tourist art and allowed his artistic talent to go to waste.

All his life, Jonathan had been propelled by a desire to show "them." In order to prove himself, it was important that he be the best in his studies, the best on the football and basketball teams. Everyone in Clearwater thought the the Sky kid was crazy when—as their town's only all-state star in ten years—he turned down a football scholarship to the University of Oklahoma and accepted one to Stanford instead.

Jonathan's own state university had chosen not to recognize the high American College Test and National Merit scores of the Indian athlete. The university wanted him only as a running back. His academic potential did not interest them. All they expected scholastically out of athletes was that they maintain their academic elegibility to play sports.

When Jonathan decided on Stanford, he had seen the disappointment on his father's face. Billy Joe had yearned for those Saturday afternoons of sitting in the stadium on the University of Oklahoma campus, basking in the glory of his son's gridiron prowess. Billy Joe never quite forgave his son for denying him that. He died during the summer between Jonathan's senior year in college and his first year at Stanford's prestigious medical school.

Jonathan met Linney the following summer. He remembered how close he had come to giving up his goals.

He couldn't let another woman distract him from his chosen course. Not for anything. Not even the achingly lovely Beth Dunning. It wouldn't take much for him to get real crazy over her. He'd already had a good example tonight of what happened then. He set himself up for a fall. Jonathan realized that now Dr. Christenson would be watching him like a hawk, waiting for the next blunder on his part. It didn't take too many blunders in the highly competitive residency program to be excused from it.

However, when he closed his eyes, Beth was still there. Jonathan seriously considered pulling on his whites and going over to the hospital pharmacy for a sleeping pill. He had never taken a sleeping pill in his life, but how else was he going to stop himself from thinking about her?

He was on call, though. A sleeping pill was out of the question. It would not do for him to be groggy if he were called to tend a patient. Of course, he was going to be groggy in the morning anyway if he didn't get some sleep.

Jonathan was painfully aware that lovesickness was not conducive to the practice of medicine.

And lovesickness was a condition of the heart for which modern medicine had no cure.

Chapter Four

It had been a strained afternoon. They had their Sunday dinner in the formal dining room as usual. In the year since Justin died, Beth and her stepdaughter, Tricia, had taken their meals in the breakfast room or in front of the kitchen television set. But on special-occasion days or when Tricia's grandmother came for her every-other-Sunday visits, they used the elegant room that had been the scene of family meals when Justin was alive. And the first anniversary of Justin's death had fallen on one of Grace Dunning's biweekly visits.

Neither Beth nor her mother-in-law nor her stepdaughter acknowledged to one another what day it was. But Beth knew the significance of the day weighed as heavily on their minds as it did on hers.

After dinner, Beth helped Tricia with the dishes and then walked about the yard with her mother-in-law. Beth enjoyed showing her flowers to Grace before the older woman drove back to Oceanside, where she made her home. Later, without really intending to be there, Beth found herself pouring a glass of brandy from the decanter in Justin's study. Funny, Beth thought. This is where she came the day that he died, to the room that represented Justin Dunning more than any other room in the house. When he was alive, Beth seldom came here. But the night of his death she had seated herself in the leather wing chair that only he used and had tried to comprehend that her husband was really gone. It was difficult for her to accept. Justin had been a larger-than-life figure. Almost Godlike. The center around which her life and so many other lives had turned. It seemed incomprehensible that such a man could have died like a mere mortal.

Although when she found Justin floating facedown in their swimming pool, Beth was frightened, she never truly considered that the ghastly episode would not end well. She had somehow managed to pull his body to the shallow end of the pool and drag him up the steps, all the time shouting for help. She administered mouth-to-mouth resuscitation alternately with cardiac massage, knowing that it was only a matter of time before her husband's body stirred. He would cough a few times, take a few minutes to clear his head and then, once revived, become again the powerful presence that dominated her life. Beth even wondered, as she exhaled air into his lungs, how he would feel about his wife having saved his life. Would he be grateful? Being grateful was not something Justin had much practice with. He was more often the one to whom people were grateful.

Her calls for help brought a frightened Tricia, who summoned the rescue squad. It seemed an eternity until the paramedics arrived, but later she was informed it had taken less than five minutes. Her body's own oxygen supply depleted, Beth was faint and trembling from her resuscitation efforts. She went with

Justin in the ambulance to the hospital, fear shaking her confidence but still believing that somehow his silent, ashen form would revive. It was just a matter of time. He was in the hands of professionals now.

But he didn't revive. He was pronounced dead on arrival at the hospital. She later learned from the autopsy report that Justin had suffered a massive heart attack—that he had not died of drowning at all—and that all the CPR in the world probably would not have saved him. Dr. Justin Dunning had succumbed to a massive coronary occlusion. He had been killed by the failure of the very organ that had brought him such prestige and fame. So ironic.

Later that night, after a sedated Tricia had finally fallen into a fitful sleep and Grace had been escorted home by her sisters, Beth had come to this room. In search of what? She didn't know, but maybe if she sat in his leather chair, she could believe the reality of Justin's death. Only Justin sat in that chair. Whenever Beth came into this room, she sat on the sofa. Never in the chair.

And a year later, on the anniversary of that day, she was here again.

The chair was thronelike, with a high back and winged sides. Beth leaned her head back and sipped at the French brandy. The brandy was fantastic, of course. Justin would have had nothing but the best. The whole room said that of him.

Beth could almost feel his presence even after a year. His books, his awards, his collection of Western and Indian art, were there. The huge desk that had once served his physician father filled one end of the room. The hunting trophies, with their frozen expressions and lifelike eyes, hung on the wall above the fireplace. All of it was the essence of Justin. Was it her imagination, or did the room still smell of his pipe tobacco?

One year a widow. One year trying to decide what to do about the rest of her life. Had the past year been an eternity or had it passed in a blur? Beth couldn't decide. It had a timeless feel about it. She simply got up in the mornings, did what she had to do during the day and went to bed at night. Time had little relevance. But now, as she sat in Justin's regal chair, sipping his brandy, she realized she had been simply biding her time, waiting for this day. One year was somehow magical, a landmark. After a year, society and one's own emotions were allowed to ease the restrictions placed by widowhood. It was time to get on with her life.

What a strange year it had been trying to bring some order to Justin's chaotic financial affairs and to make ends meet that simply wouldn't. A year of learning how to maintain a huge house with little paid help, of continuing with her various hospital-related responsibilities which, oddly, seemed to increase rather than decrease after her husband's death, and of dealing with a confusing set of emotions.

"So what now?" Beth asked, raising her glass to the elk head mounted on the opposite wall. "What are you and I going to do? I hate to tell you this, old fellow, but you may be looking for a new home. If I can't figure out some way to pay a few bills, we both may be out on the street."

And now what about Jonathan Sky? Beth wondered. What did the arrival of the young surgeon in her life mean? She only knew that the fact that she would see Jonathan tonight had helped her manage to survive this grim anniversary day.

Beth rose from the chair and crossed the room to refill her glass. She wondered if she was drinking too much these days. She did use a nightcap to help her sleep at night. Was that a danger sign? She picked up the lead-crystal decanter and stared at it, wondering what it would be worth if she sold it. But then, she wasn't free to sell it. According to the terms of Justin's will, she shared ownership of the house and its contents with her stepdaughter. Tricia was a minor, and her share of her father's estate was to be held in trust until she was twenty-one.

She poured only one finger of brandy this time. She started to return to the leather chair but decided against it. She should go check on Tricia and see how her stepdaughter was dealing with the anniversary of her father's death.

Beth stopped underneath the elk head and stared up at him. She had never liked having the head of a dead animal on the wall. Why did a man whose job it was to save lives want to have trophies of death on his walls? It occurred to her for the first time, that she didn't have to live with the stuffed animal heads. There was no reason why everything had to remain just as Justin had left it. Yet even after one year of being on her own, she was finding it difficult to make decisions based solely on what she thought best or on what she wanted. In many ways Justin's personality and influence still held sway over her life. She wondered sometimes if it would always be so.

She started for the door, then looked back at the assortment of animal heads with their fixed, glassy eyes. This was *her* house now, she thought with an uncharacteristic rush of defiance.

"I hope you don't mind," she said to the elk, "but I think your new home will be in the attic if I can find someone to help me get you and your friends down from the walls. Nothing personal, I assure you. Well, *ciao*. It's been nice visiting with you, but I need to go see how Tricia is getting along."

As Beth started up the wide staircase, she looked down at the brandy snifter in her hand. She paused, then walked down the central hallway to the kitchen. The brandy left an oily film on the bottom of the sink when Beth dumped it out. She ran water over it and put the glass in the dishwasher.

When the phone rang, her heart skipped a beat. It had an annoying habit of doing that these days. But she couldn't help it. Each time the phone rang, she hoped it would be Jonathan's voice she would hear when she picked up the receiver.

But it was a wrong number.

Beth was irritated at the blanket of disappointment that enveloped her. She shrugged it off.

Tricia was lying on her bed, an opened book beside her. Her room decor was that of a typical teenager. Posters of rock stars decorated the walls, a bulletin board laden with mementos hung over her ruffled bed, and stuffed animals left over from childhood lined a shelf above her desk.

"You okay?" Beth asked, sitting down on the side of the bed.

"Yes and no. I miss Daddy, but sometimes I miss the things that will never happen more than I miss what actually did. Does that make any sense at all?"

"Yes, indeed. I feel the same way. Maybe death wouldn't be so sad if when it came everything was tidy, if we had said all the things that needed to be said to that person, if we had shared all the good experiences that were meant to be shared. But I think death is almost always an interruption. It seldom comes at an appropriate time."

Tricia sat up, hugging a pillow to her chest. "I'm glad we have each other," she said. "Sometimes I get afraid of losing you."

"I can't promise not to die, Tricia. But I promise I'll try to hang in there till I'm old. And I promise that as long as I'm alive, you'll be my beloved daughter."

Tricia bit her lip and nodded.

"How about a walk on the beach?" Beth asked.

"Okay," Tricia said slowly.

They stopped in the kitchen to get some stale bread to feed the gulls. The phone rang just as they opened the back door on their way to the beach. Beth picked up the kitchen extension. This time it was Jonathan.

"I can't make it this evening," he said. "I've got to assist Dr. Bernard. He's located a donor heart for one of his patients."

"I understand," Beth said. And she did. She understood that patients came first. But that did not keep her from feeling jilted. "How about tomorrow evening?" he asked. "I have the emergency room, but not until eleven. I could bring along some Chinese food or a pizza." His voice was hopeful.

"Tomorrow evening? That would be fine," Beth said. The eagerness in her voice matched his.

He really wanted to see her. Beth felt giddy. Then she looked at Tricia. The look on her stepdaughter's face told her something. Tomorrow was Monday. She and Tricia had planned to go down to Old Town tomorrow evening—to wander through the museums and shops and eat Mexican food in their favorite restaurant. It was less crowded with tourists on Mondays.

"No, Jonathan, wait," Beth said almost frantically. "I can't. I have other plans."

Tricia was very quiet as they walked along the beach. Even the antics of the gulls didn't seem to cheer her. Usually she threw the bread high in the air for the gulls to catch in mid-flight. But today she opened the bag and dumped it out on the beach.

They stood for a time watching the greedy birds dart about, grabbing bread out of each other's beaks. "Let's go to a movie," Beth suggested.

"I think I'd rather just read," Tricia said.

THAT BETH WAS STILL ALIVE, that she had lived to see her twentieth and subsequent birthdays, was a miracle—a miracle provided by the man who later became her husband.

Justin had saved her life. That knowledge had been with her every day of her life for the past ten years. She would be dead if it weren't for Justin. Without his incredibly dramatic intervention, her life would have ended two weeks before her twentieth birthday. How did one ever repay a debt like that? Justin himself died before Beth could find an answer to that question. She often thought how tidy it would have been if the CPR had worked there by the swimming pool—if she had been able to revive Justin. Then she would have saved his life, and the debt would have been paid. Maybe that would have changed things between them.

But she had not saved Justin's life. He had died, and the debt would never be repaid. She would always owe everything to him.

Before her surgery, Beth had never been robust. She had suffered from what her father called "delicate health." Beth's mother had been a fragile woman, so it didn't seem strange that Beth seemed to have inherited her mother's weak constitution. At one point, Beth was diagnosed as having a heart murmur, but her parents were told not to worry—that she would most likely outgrow it. In the meantime, the elderly French physician who cared for the family cautioned Beth's parents that they were to see she avoided physical activity. A more up-to-date physician might have handled Beth's case differently. Beth's less-than-robust body was made even more fragile by a lack of physical exercise.

Beth's childhood memories were of a mother who was always resting and of an active, athletic father who was frequently off on some diplomatic assignment in a far corner of the globe. Beth had been raised by various French or Swiss housekeepers. She spent most of her time reading.

Her mother died when Beth was thirteen, but not of her vaguely defined "condition." She was struck by a car as she came out of a restaurant. At the time, Beth's father was a career diplomat based in Switzerland. Beth spent the rest of her school years in a girls' boarding school near Lucerne. Her father remarried a French woman and had two rosy-faced little sons by the time Beth graduated from secondary school. Beth was sent to California to live with her mother's sister and attend UCLA.

It was her Aunt Megan who simply refused to attribute Beth's frail body and lack of stamina to having inherited her mother's weak constitution.

"Your mother was an alcoholic," Megan said bluntly. "I don't know what your problem is, but I think it's a crying shame no one found out before now."

Megan's quest took her and Beth to San Diego and the office of Dr. Justin Dunning, already a recognized name in and out of medical circles. Justin was forty-one at the time, a lion of a man who seemed to be alternately feared and respected by the entourage of young physicians who always accompanied him on his rounds.

Beth was diagnosed as having a congenital subaortic stenosis—a narrowing of the aorta, which was the main trunk of the system of arteries responsible for taking oxygenated blood to all limbs and organs except the lungs. In Beth's body, this giant vein was prevented from adequately doing its job by a narrowing, or stenosis, just above the celiac artery.

Justin Dunning advised surgery to correct the anomaly. Beth didn't immediately call her father about the problem, as Dr. Dunning advised. Instead, she decided that she would wait and talk it over with him when she visited him during her Christmas vacation. She was afraid he would insist she have the surgery immediately, before she completed her first semester of college. But she wasn't actually sick, Beth reasoned. The artery had apparently always been narrowed. She would follow the mild exercise program Dr. Dunning recommended and see how things went. Maybe she would improve without surgery.

In the meantime, she continued her studies. She did well in her classes, but each day when they were over, she wearily returned to her aunt's home. She was not a part of campus life. There were no dates. Beth was too shy to join any clubs and too socially inexperienced to know how to respond to the young men who would tentatively flirt with her. And by the end of the day, she was often too tired to attend club meetings or lectures. She did her studies and went to bed. That this was not the normal life-style of a college coed was not something to which Beth gave much thought. She had always lived a quiet, sheltered life. She had always tired easily. The life she was leading seemed normal for her.

Beth was scheduled to fly to France in order to spend the Christmas break with her father and her stepfamily. Her aunt drove her to the airport. Later, when Beth looked back on that drive, she found it ironic that she had joked with Megan about the rash of hijackings plaguing the airlines. Or perhaps by joking about it people deny the possibility of their ever having such an experience. Perhaps many people about to embark on a journey by air that day made a lighthearted comment about a side trip to Havana, for in doing so, they somehow reassured themselves that such things could only happen to other people. It was the sort of thing you hear about on the news, an abstraction that had nothing to do with you yourself.

That's how Beth and her fellow passengers still felt when the three Cubans commandeered the plane during the St. Louis to New York segment of their journey. People frowned and looked at one another in disbelief as the pilot explained to them over the public address system that some "gentlemen" were insisting he fly the plane to Havana. This can only happen to other people, she thought. Maybe it was just a drill to test people's reactions—a research project by the airlines or the government. It didn't feel like a hijacking.

The flight attendants, looking strained but still smiling, served drinks and reassured the passengers as best they could.

The coast of Florida slid past them, and soon they did indeed land in Havana.

While Cuban officials worked on making arrangements to return the plane and its passengers to the States, the passengers were cloistered in a barnlike room furnished only with ancient wooden benches. Beth tried to stretch out on one of the benches, but lying down with no pillow caused pressure on her chest and took her breath away. She tried using her purse for a pillow, but that only partially relieved the problem. Still it was hard for her to breathe. She tried to lie on her side but finally gave up and spent the endless night in a sitting position.

Totally miserable, she vowed to discuss the operation Dr. Dunning had recommended with her father. She was frightened by her shortness of breath. Never had it been so acute. And when she looked in the mirror of her compact, her lips looked blue. She covered them with lipstick and prayed that morning would come soon.

But morning brought only more waiting. It was the next afternoon before the passengers were escorted back to the airplane, which was to be flown the short distance to Miami, the passengers were told. From there they would be booked into hotels and then worked into flights the next day to take them to their original destinations.

That evening, the national news showed the tired passengers from Havana arriving at Miami International Airport. As the passengers disembarked from the plane, an NBC-affiliate reporter thrust his microphone in front of the exhausted-looking Beth.

"Were you afraid for your life?" the reporter asked without preliminaries.

Beth made a valiant attempt to answer. But the words did not come easily. She did not feel well at all. She was exhausted from lack of sleep. Every muscle in her body ached. And she simply could not get her breath. How was she ever going to manage the transatlantic flight to Europe? But she had to go. She had to tell her father about the operation. Suddenly her carry-on bag was too heavy for her to hold one more second. The words she spoke into the microphone were mumbled.

"No, I never felt that I was in any real danger," she said as best she could. But it was hard to talk and breathe at the same time.

"Excuse me?" the reporter asked. "Would you mind repeating that."

"Real danger," Beth repeated with a gasp. Then she gave up and waved him away. "I'm sorry."

Justin Dunning watched the five-thirty news on the television in the physician's lounge as he changed back into his street clothes. The live interview from Miami caught his attention. He didn't remember her name, but he recognized the young woman. Subaortic stenosis. Obviously she'd never had the surgery he recommended. Justin watched as she paused to put her carry-on bag on the floor, then almost fell as she tried to regain a standing posture. He watched her struggle for breath, attempting to answer the reporter's question. Of course, the ashen cast to her coloring could simply be in the television adjustment, but unless he missed his bet, she was in acute congestive failure right now.

Dr. Dunning made a series of phone calls to the Miami airport, to the company owning the hijacked airliner and to the television station that ran the hijacking story. He discovered the passengers had been taken to spend the night at several different hotels near the airport. It was at this point that Justin tried to enlist the aid of the Miami Police Department. But his story about diagnosing conjestive heart failure via a transcontinental television broadcast was met with less-than-tolerant skepticism by the various police officials to whom he spoke. The more arrogant and demanding Justin became, the less interested the police seemed in his story.

"Look, doctor," the officer who was handling his call said in a voice that insinuated he doubted if Justin really deserved the title, "if the lady is sick, she can ask for help. We do have doctors in Miami. And we don't dragnet the city in search of people who look sick on television. Right now we've got a hostage situation at a motel, a killing at a liquor store, a potential suicide who wants to take a leap from a twelfth-floor ledge and a ten-vehicle pileup to occupy our time."

Aware that he was being dismissed as "just another kook," Justin canceled his plans for the evening and drove incredibly fast to the airport. He caught a night flight out of San Diego without so much as a minute to spare. It was just after two in the morning when he appeared at the airport office in Miami and demanded to be taken to the young woman who had appeared on the news broadcast.

Justin Dunning, in person, commanded attention. He assumed authority as if it were his God-given right. He was used to people hopping to attention when he came into the room. He was used to getting results. An airline official escorted him to a nearby hotel.

The hotel management took a little convincing when Beth did not answer the phone in her room. The lady was probably out for a late night on the town, celebrating her safe return from a hijacking, they said. Finally, however, with a policeman and hotel security officer in attendance, an assistant manager opened the door to Beth's room. She was unconscious—and blue. None of those who entered her hotel room had any further doubts as to the accuracy of the California heart surgeon's transcontinental diagnosis.

Justin, with the help of a court order giving him temporary operating rights, bullied his way into the Greater Miami Medical Center. With the help of a few well-placed threats from Justin about legal liability and damaging publicity, the hospital assembled a surgery crew for the California surgeon in record time. Word traveled fast around the medical center. *The* Justin Dunning. Operating here. Emergency valve replacement. By the time the operation began, there was standing room only in the overhead spectators' area. The disgruntled hospital administration was initially upset over this disregard of their rules—until they realized the media potential of this dramatic surgery. In spite of the early-morning hour, the remote units from local television stations soon were parked in the hospital parking lot. A waiting room was turned over to media representatives, who had no trouble finding the background they needed on the glamorous Dr. Justin Dunning. But they had little information on his mystery patient, other than that she had been on the hijacked aircraft.

But the reporters' fancies were definitely tickled. The great heart surgeon diagnosing a life-threatening heart condition via a transcontinental television newscast! And then flying across the country to save the young woman, who was beautiful by all reports. So much the better. Handsome heart surgeon dramatically saves beautiful young woman. Great story! Reports of the surgery in progress were carried on *Today* and *Good Morning America*.

When the hospital's buoyant chief administrator announced that the surgery had concluded and that the patient was doing beautifully, the assembled media broke into spontaneous applause before rushing off to phone in or film their reports. And later that day, when Dr. Dunning held his press conference, it was to a packed hospital auditorium. After Justin was introduced, he received a lengthy standing ovation from media representatives, who put aside their normally blasé, objective affectation and clapped and cheered their appreciation of a good story and a happy ending.

Evening papers all across the country carried the story. By then, Beth had been identified as a UCLA coed. Her aunt was besieged by reporters as she raced through the Los Angeles airport to catch a plane to rush to her stricken niece's side.

"Yes," Megan told the reporters, "my niece has a heart condition. Dr. Dunning had recommended surgery some months ago. We should have listened to him."

So Beth had been the famous doctor's patient before all this happened. How interesting, decided an innovative woman reporter from a national tabloid whose editorial policies did not include the truth. The reporter quickly determined that Dr. Dunning was a widower and immediately prefabricated her sensationalized feature story on the dramatic surgery. Its headline read, "Famous Surgeon Rescues Ladylove from Certain Death." UCLA had not been able to supply a picture of Beth, but the undaunted reporter had determined where she went to secondary school and miraculously procured from the Swiss school—which in the article was referred to as a convent school—a picture of Beth taken for the school yearbook. Beth, like all her classmates, had been photographed in her white graduation dress. Beth's hair fell across one shoulder. Her throat was encircled by a string of pearls. The reflection of the photographer's lights made stars in her brown eyes. Her mouth was captured in a soft, vulnerable smile. She looked dewy-fresh and innocent.

Refusing to be topped, the front-page headline of the competing national tabloid carried a headline that read, "Modern-Day Prince Charming Saves His Fairy Princess from Death's Door." Their story hinted that Beth was enrolled incognito at UCLA and that she was really the daughter of an exiled monarch of a European principality. They pirated the schoolgirl picture of Beth from the competition, but when they ran it, the pearls had miraculously changed to emeralds, and a diamond tiara rested on Beth's head.

The account that appeared in *Time* magazine was more accurate, but even the prestigious news magazine could not resist the romantic touch. Dunning had gone back to Los Angeles after Beth's surgery but returned to Miami for his patient's first public appearance. Justin himself pushed Beth's wheelchair into the auditorium for the press conference. When he leaned forward to say something to her, the *Time* photographer captured the fairy-tale couple. Beth's face was lifted toward her handsome savior. Her lips were slightly parted. Their mouths were only inches apart. Justin's hand was resting protectively on her slender, robed shoulder. In reality, Beth had been commenting on the number of reporters in the room and stating her nervousness, but in the resulting photograph they appeared to be sharing an intimacy.

When Beth's turn at the microphone came, she tearfully stated her gratitude toward Justin. "I owe my life to Dr. Justin Dunning," Beth said. "He will forever be my hero."

The caption of the *Time*'s photograph read, "Hero physician receives accolades from grateful patient."

And indeed it had been hero worship for Beth from the beginning. For her, the entire experience had been as romantic as the tabloids portrayed it. Their facts were wrong, but the drama and romance were indeed the modern-day fairy tale portrayed by the media. Justin Dunning was a knight in shining armor who had flown to her rescue, and Beth felt like a royal princess. She clipped out all the articles and pasted them in a scrapbook. She stared for long hours at the *Time* magazine photograph of herself with the great physician. The sight of his hand resting on her shoulder left her a little dizzy. He had touched her there,

Beth thought as she touched her own right shoulder where Justin's hand had once rested.

When Justin started courting her, she was deeply honored as well as compellingly flattered by his attention. He was handsome, wealthy, famous, respected and had saved her life—a powerful list of credentials to an inexperienced twenty-year-old woman who didn't understand the difference between gratitude and love, between hero worship and love.

Even their subsequent wedding had a fairy-tale feel about it for Beth. Her aunt made Beth a dress fit for a princess. Many of Justin's celebrity friends and patients were in attendance, including several movie stars—Southern California's version of royalty. Beth's father even came to the wedding and was obviously proud that a man of Justin Dunning's stature had chosen his daughter as his wife. The wedding was held in the oceanside garden of Justin's elegant La Jolla home. A string quartet furnished the music. The champagne spouted forth from a sterling fountain. The scent of gardenias and hyacinths filled the air.

The fairy tale ended for Beth on her wedding night. Justin was quick and brusque in his dispensation of her virginity. Beth wasn't quite sure just what she was supposed to feel in her marital bed, but she knew she had not experienced it. And she assumed the shortcoming was hers, a feeling that persisted even after she intellectually came to realize that Justin might be her husband but he was not a caring lover. Sex to him was nothing more than a physiological response that required expression. He was not a sensual person. No passion resided in his manly breast. It either did not occur to him that Beth might want or need something more, or it simply did not concern him. Or perhaps, as Beth eventually decided, it was a combination of both factors. But regardless of the exact reason, she was married to a man who approached sex in the same way he approached eating breakfast. He wanted an egg, milk and orange juice mixed in the blender and ready for him to gulp down on his way out the door in the morning. No fuss. No bother. No anticipation of any special treat—just the same fare every day. No lingering. No intimate conversation. No excitement. Justin dispensed with both sex and breakfast as efficiently as possible.

Not that he didn't care for his young wife in his own way. Beth understood that. And she also realized that aside from any caring, her husband also looked upon her as an image enhancer. The whole Beth episode, including their courtship and marriage, had brought him an incredible amount of goodwill and media attention. Anyone who had not heard of him or his work before certainly had by now. No publicist could have dreamed up anything in a million years that could have done more for the Dunning recognition factor than that episode. And no one was more aware than Justin of the importance of the recognition factor. People had to know who he was before they could help him make his dream come true. And his dream was to create a glorious future for the Healing Arts Medical Center. His own medical kingdom. A medical center that was privately financed so he was not working at the whim of university administrators or government bureaucrats. Instead of scrapping for grant money to conduct research, Healing Arts would itself become one of the country's major grant-giving foundations subsidizing cardiovascular research.

Beth had been a treasure chest of goodwill and feminine virtue. She was gradually beginning to understand that the shortcomings in her relationship with her husband had not been soley her fault except in the sense of her powerlessness to effect a change. If she had been a different sort of person, more experienced and more sensual, maybe she could have built a better relationship with him. But she rather suspected that her lack of those traits was the reason he wanted to marry her in the first place. A person unaccustomed to passion—or incapable of it—didn't expect much out of the physical side of marriage.

But the lack of passion on her part did not make her any less subject to Justin's power. She was no match for her husband's indomitable will. She slipped into his shadow and stayed there until he died nine years later.

Because she owed Justin her life, in a sense Beth felt that she belonged to him. She was too young and inexperienced to consider her own rights in the matter. And then there was Justin's daughter, Tricia—a neglected, lonely child still suffering from the death of her mother eighteen months before Beth came into her life. While marriage had been a disappointment to Beth, her new role as Tricia's stepmother was the most rewarding of her life. The two formed an instantaneous bond born out of their mutual need. Beth soon loved the six-year-old with the fierce dedication of a natural mother. Tricia was the joy in an otherwise joyless day. Tricia blossomed under Beth's love.

As wisdom began to slip into Beth's soul, she came to understand that her love for Tricia was a trap that held her in an impossible marriage—that and the debt she could never repay. She owed both her life and her beloved stepdaughter to Justin. And divorcing Justin would mean losing Tricia.

Beth assumed the duties associated with raising his daughter gladly. With a quiet efficiency amazing for one so young, she ran her husband's household and his social and civic life. In spite of the problems of the bedroom, Beth wanted Justin's respect and praise and worked hard to achieve it.

The few times Beth dared to launch a discussion of their sexual adjustment, Justin skillfully managed to indicate that he considered any shortcoming to be hers.

"Some women just don't have any capacity to enjoy sex," he explained.

Thus avoiding sex became a way of life for Beth. She avoided undressing in front of her husband and any sort of physical contact with him. Nor did she wear any revealing clothing. She took care not to accidentally brush against him in the night. Even though he was usually up and on his way to the hospital by six o'clock in the morning, Beth always tried to be out of bed before the alarm clock went off in order to avoid the possibility of any early-morning intimacy.

As the years went by, she continued to think from time to time of divorce. When Tricia went off to college would be the appropriate time. But Beth wasn't sure if she could ever leave Justin. In his way, he really needed her. And a physical relationship was just part of a marriage, she kept telling herself. After all, he treated her well at other times, denied her nothing and seemed quite happy with their marriage. "I don't know what I would do without you," Justin would often acknowledge sincerely for her having paid careful attention to the details of his life and freeing him to concentrate on his profession. In recent years, she even filled in for him at public appearances when he could not keep commitments. People, it seemed, would never forget the drama of Justin's courtship of her and loved to glean any detail they could about the romantic story. They were always fascinated to meet Beth in person.

Beth never tried to be anything more than Justin's wife when she was called on to represent him. She was always careful to speak for Justin, making an appeal for whatever charity or cause was being espoused—usually the Healing Arts Foundation. She never overstepped unspoken boundaries or attempted to establish her own identity. She understood the unwritten rules. She was accepted only because of the person to whom she was married. As an individual, her views mattered not at all. She was Mrs. Justin Dunning. To those who had known his first wife, she was the second Mrs. Justin Dunning. Like an interchangeable part, she stepped into the shoes, the role and the identity of her predecessor. She, like the woman before her, lived in her husband's shadow.

And she lived in fear. No matter how she tried to rationalize, no matter how she tried to convince herself that a wife should be able to put up with an occasional unpleasantness in the marital bed in exchange for her husband's support and admiration, she came to dread her husband's touch for what it might lead to. She simply did not enjoy the physical part of her marriage. But as Justin had pointed out, some women just didn't enjoy sex.

Chapter Five

Dr. Morrison stood looking out the window, his back to Jonathan.

"The foundation to the new wing is almost completed," Morrison commented, his tone filled with satisfaction. Jonathan could hear, drifting in through the closed window, the sounds of heavy machinery and the warning bell of concrete trucks backing up. He could visualize the huge crane lifting prefabricated slabs into place and the continuous convoy of trucks that came onto the construction site each day, dumping their load between preset forms and lumbering off again for another.

"They'll start up with it soon," the hospital administrator said with a bobbing of his head, as though agreeing with his own statement. He turned to face Jonathan and stood with his hands behind his back. "Six stories," he continued. "A hundred thousand square feet housing the most comprehensive facility for cardiovascular research in a private sector in the entire country. Justin's dream continues to come true. He said Healing Arts would be a great medical center—an independent center free to pursue whatever lines of research its scientists and clinicians deem appropriate. And to be that sort of facility, you have to pave new roads. Justin always said you have to be unfettered and prepared. But you don't get out in front or stay there without money."

The words sounded familiar to Jonathan. He had heard them before at hospital staff meetings, at the ground-breaking ceremonies for the new wing, at the Christmas party for the resident staff.

Morrison returned to his spacious desk and lowered his considerable bulk into the large leather chair. "The Wishart family," he continued, "has endowed almost half the cost of this building in recognition of Justin's successful heart-transplant surgery on their daughter, their only child. She lived four more years because of the donor heart Justin gave her."

Morrison leaned forward and took a sip from the cup of coffee that rested on a small cup-sized hot plate on his desk. Jonathan followed suit and took a sip of his. But his coffee was tepid, and Jonathan returned it to the saucer. He'd had enough this morning anyway. What he needed was breakfast. Or he guessed lunch would be more appropriate at this hour. But he was scheduled to operate during the lunch hour, so a candy bar would have to do. Funny how doctors tell other people to take care of their bodies and so often don't pay any attention to their own advice. But even a candy bar sounded wonderful right now. Then maybe he could stomach some more coffee.

He tried to forget about his raw stomach and returned his attention to Morrison's droning voice. "The Cynthia Wishart Memorial Research Wing is very important to her parents," Morrison was saying as though addressing a roomful of people and not just one impatient resident who needed to get back to work

and wanted the man to hurry up and make his point.
"The building symbolizes their faith in the work that
is being done at Healing Arts and their confidence in
the future of organ transplants. It is their gift to other
parents so that they might be able to see their stricken
children grow to adulthood."

As though seeking inspiration from the sight, Morrison swiveled his chair around to look out the window again. "The Wisharts are quite intent on having
the Justin Dunning Medical Research Library stand as
a tribute to their daughter's physician," he continued. "They envision it as someday housing the most
important resources on the history of cardiovascular
research in the nation. They stand ready to supply the
money to make that library the envy of all other such
facilities in the world, and they want the library to include Justin's personal papers. The library must present a retrospective of the career of the man they
honor. Those papers need to be cataloged with great
care by someone who not only has the medical
knowledge to understand them but also has enough
literary perspective to assemble the book that Mrs.
Dunning wants."

Morrison wasn't saying anything that Jonathan
hadn't already heard. He realized that the older
doctor's words were simply the preparatory rhetoric
leading up to a point he was about to make. So Jonathan recrossed his legs, tried not to appear impatient
and waited.

"I fully realize, Doctor," Morrison said, looking
directly at Jonathan now and not addressing a roomful of imaginary people, "that cataloging all those
papers will be a large chore, and the compiling of the
book according to Mrs. Dunning's wishes an even

more challenging task, but you are very capable. And you do have a vacation coming up. You indicated when we last spoke with the Wisharts that you might be willing to devote your vacation to this project and that the stipend we offered was satisfactory. I find it difficult to believe that your financial ills have magically healed themselves in the past week. So I find myself puzzled over your request to withdraw from the project." Morrison picked up a letter opener and held it end to end between his forefingers. He was silent, apparently giving Jonathan a chance to reply and correct any misconceptions.

Jonathan said nothing, however, waiting for the punch line of this entire scenario. He had a pretty good idea what it was going to be.

"Mr. and Mrs. Wishart like you, Jonathan," Morrison continued. "Her mother, as I told you, traces her heritage to California's Pomo tribe. She was absolutely charmed at the idea of having someone of Indian blood involved in this project, and she and her husband have already announced your participation to the press. It would be difficult to explain to the Wisharts that you have decided to withdraw. But before you make a final decision about the library project, let me point out that Dr. Christenson has voiced reservations about your being named chief resident this fall and being accepted into the cardiovascular surgery fellowship the following year. As you know, it is getting close to time for the chief resident to be selected, and whoever is selected for that high honor would most assuredly advance into the fellowship program. You can assume that you will not have Christenson's support on this matter. But there are others involved in the selective process, and I think that these individuals would consider your continuing on the Dunning project as a sign of your dedication to Healing Arts.''

Jonathan got the message.

What Morrison was really saying was "Play ball on this and I'll support you for the chief residency." Jonathan knew he could not afford to lose Morrison's support.

Jonathan met Dr. Morrison's challenging gaze, then stood up and extended his hand. "You will reconsider your decision?" Morrison asked anxiously.

"Do I have a choice?" Jonathan asked, and, without waiting for an answer, took his leave of the hospital chief of staff.

As he made his way along the tunnellike corridors back to the surgery wing, he wondered why he didn't feel more distressed about the outcome of his meeting with Dr. Morrison. He had gone to see the hospital administrator about withdrawing from the Dunning project. He had come to realize that the project and Beth Dunning would be great distractions in his life—distractions he could ill afford.

But Morrison would have none of his quitting. Jonathan realized that a little not-so-subtle blackmail had just been applied to him. Morrison's message was clear. "You do the Dunning papers, and I'll keep you out of harm's way." In this instance, harm came in the form of a surgeon named Christenson and others involved in a power struggle within the medical center hierarchy.

So why wasn't he mad? Jonathan asked himself as he returned a student nurse's smile with one of his own and an uncharacteristic wink. He should be hot under the collar right now over being forced to spend his valuable time on a project of which he no longer wished to be a part.

But he wasn't mad. In fact, he felt damned good. He felt so good, he broke into a jog and passed by other slower-moving people in the long hallway.

The answer, of course, was that at least part of his decision concerning Beth Dunning had been made for him. The situation in which he found himself forced him to continue with the project. If he didn't, Morrison would not support him against Christenson. And Christenson was certainly acting as if he were planning to make trouble. He wanted his own protégés to advance into the cardiovascular program. He wanted to be the next Justin Dunning. And he had a vendetta against Jonathan.

He needed Morrison on his side, Jonathan reasoned almost gleefully. So whether or not he should see Beth anymore was out of his hands. He had to see her. He would be going to her house. He would be spending time with her. The thought both excited and terrified him. He wanted to see her again. There was no point in kidding himself anymore. But he feared where it would lead. He feared the power of his attraction to the lovely young widow with the sad brown eyes.

BETH STARED at her reflection in the full-length mirror. She looked plain, and that wasn't how she wanted to look at all.

She took off the white blouse and navy suit skirt she had just put on and returned them to her closet. She stared at her wardrobe in disgust. You'd think some old woman owned those clothes, she thought. Proper little dresses suitable for afternoon teas and early-evening receptions hung neatly on one side. And on the other side of the closet there were clothes to wear around the house—jeans and the like, along with a few ordinary-looking sundresses that suddenly looked faded and out of style. There was nothing that might be considered current or stylish. There was nothing in which she would feel young and confident and attractive for a casual evening working in Justin's study with Jonathan Sky.

She reached for a pair of black slacks fresh from the cleaners still in its plastic bag. *It really doesn't matter,* she told herself. *Just get dressed.* The slacks suited her fine last week.

Beth paired the slacks with a white-knit shell and pink cardigan sweater, then surveyed herself in the mirror. She added a string of pearls. She looked about as chic as a bag lady, she decided. The slacks were stretched out at the knees and too big in the waist. The sweater was just that—a sweater. Utilitarian. The sort of thing you put on because you were chilly, not because you needed to look good.

On a whim, she went down the hall to Tricia's room. Her stepdaughter was sprawled across her bed with her homework spread out around her.

"Care if I borrow that yellow skirt with the big pockets?" Beth asked.

"No. Where are you going?"

"No place. Dr. Sky is coming over here to work some more on your father's papers. My wardrobe seems to consist of nothing but old blue jeans—or proper little navy-blue crepe dresses and conservative beige gabardine suits. I haven't bought anything new in so long. I want something casual and at-home-looking without having to resort to one of my washed-

out cotton sundresses." Beth realized she was giving
more of an explanation than was necessary, but she
felt she had to document her need in front of her
stepdaughter. Although she didn't want Tricia to think
her meeting with Jonathan Sky was anything special,
the words flowed on. "I thought maybe a cotton skirt
with a blouse might be appropriate. I do have that
yellow-and-white striped camp shirt or that navy pullover made like your red one. Either top would look
good with your yellow shirt, don't you think?"

Tricia stared at Beth for a minute. "You're dressing up special for him?" she asked, her voice suspicious.

"No more than I would for anyone else who
dropped by in the evening." Beth said, thinking how
stupid her words sounded. No one ever "dropped by
in the evening" to see her. Tricia's friends dropped by.
But Beth and Justin's friends had always come by in-
vitation only. What to wear in the evening for drop-in
guests had not been an issue in her life before. And for
invited guests she wore one of those boring navy
dresses.

"Well, you can borrow it if you want," Tricia said
sullenly, "but don't you think it's a little young for
you?"

Beth went to Tricia's closet and pulled out the skirt
in question. It was a simple gathered skirt of yellow
cotton. How could it be too young for anyone?

Could Tricia feel threatened by her stepmother's
having a man call on her? Beth started to reassure the
girl that this was strictly a business meeting, that it
wasn't a personal relationship at all. But she held
back. She wanted to reassure Tricia, but then she herself wasn't sure just what sort of relationship was de-

veloping between her and Jonathan Sky. She wasn't even sure what sort she wanted it to be.

Beth perched for a minute on the side of Tricia's bed and gave the girl a one-sided hug. "There's stuff for sandwiches in the kitchen. Dr. Sky and I will eat in your father's study. You're welcome to join us if you wish."

"No, thanks," Tricia said emphatically. "I'm going over to Kimmie's house to study. I'm invited for dinner."

"Oh?" Beth said. "Well, I'm glad I haven't cooked anything. You really should let me know ahead of time when you're not eating at home."

Tricia shrugged her indifference and turned her attention back to her homework.

Irritated, Beth took the skirt and left without closing the door behind her. Very shortly, she could hear it being slammed shut.

Beth put on a navy knit top and navy espadrilles with the yellow skirt. She put a hemp belt around her waist and tied a jaunty yellow scarf at her throat. Back to the mirror. Maybe the scarf looked too young. Tricia's comment eroded what little self-confidence she had left. She didn't want to look foolish.

Beth took off the scarf and put a single strand of small gold beads around her neck to replace it. And she placed some small gold hoops at her ears, leaving in her jewelry box the more flamboyant and larger gold loops she had planned to wear.

Tricia was leaving as Jonathan drove up. Beth watched out the open front door as her stepdaughter paused and pointedly regarded Jonathan as he emerged from his small car, then raced over to get into her girlfriend's car without offering a greeting or even a cordial nod in Jonathan's direction.

"I'm sorry," she said as Jonathan walked up the front sidewalk. "Ordinarily my daughter is polite and friendly."

"Doesn't like a man coming around to see you, I'll bet," Jonathan offered almost jokingly.

He was wearing the same tweed sport coat over freshly starched jeans and a white knit shirt. He'd had a haircut since Sunday. Beth was struck anew with the almost brutal beauty of the man. There was nothing subtle about the face of Jonathan Sky. It was strong and bold. She felt like a star-struck adolescent. She felt silly and excited and full of life—all because this man was standing before her.

He had stopped just short of the door and looked at her. Beth stood on the front step, making their faces exactly level. His eyes were the darkest, richest brown imaginable. She had spent the last three days living for this moment. Beth hadn't wanted to admit it before, but now she knew it was true. There hadn't been a moment since Sunday night when Jonathan Sky wasn't on her mind.

"I tried to get out of coming back here," he said, his joking tone of a minute before completely gone from his voice.

Beth stared at him for a minute, finding it hard to adapt to his suddenly grim demeanor. She had the feeling she'd missed something—some transition that had taken him from jovial to grim.

"Why?" Beth asked, disappointment over his words suddenly filling her throat.

"Because I'm getting hung up on you, Beth." His tone was suddenly quite hard now. "Because I'm thinking about you too much and wanting things from you I can't have. Because I'm not going to let anything stand in the way of my ambition. Because I don't have time for you or this project. I never should have let Morrison talk me into it in the first place, but I got so damned worked up over the prospect of being with you that reason did not prevail."

"And now you're sorry?" Beth said, horrified to realize there were tears lurking behind her eyes. Jonathan liked her, but the fact made him angry. She didn't know whether to be glad because he was "hung up" on her or sad because he was obviously provoked by the condition.

"Yes, very sorry," he said tersely. "I don't have room for such complications in my life. Do you realize how few native Americans ever get as far as I do in medicine?"

He didn't seem to expect an answer to his question. His voice grew hard and angry as he continued his onslaught.

"Do you realize that I will be the only American Indian cardiovascular surgeon in the country if I get through this nightmare called a residency and am allowed to do the cardiovascular fellowship? Do you realize what that means to someone who grew up an Indian in Clearwater, Oklahoma? Someone who watched his father give up on his life and art and turn into just another drunk Indian, beating a tom-tom for tourists and painting designs on Made-in-Hong-Kong peace pipes and totem poles in order to support his family? Do you know how much I want to do this for sisters and cousins and their children, for my mother, for all the others who need someone to show them what's possible, for my father, who told me on his deathbed that he died in peace knowing the son of Billy Joe Sky would vindicate his father's wasted life?''

"Why are you mad at me?" Beth said, vaguely aware the tears had escaped and were rolling down her cheeks. She wanted to run into her house and escape from this angry man.

"I'm mad because I think of you all the time and can't concentrate on my work. Because I was so excited to be coming here last Sunday night that I forgot to tell the switchboard operator where I was going and got myself into real hot water by not being available when I was needed. Because I can't sleep at night and have been walking around like a zombie all day long. Today I would have ordered the wrong dosage on a patient's medication if a sharp nurse hadn't questioned me. Because you're so damned beautiful it makes my heart turn over just to look at you. Because I want to kiss you and hold and make love to you. Damn it, Beth, I'm losing myself over you.''

She didn't know she was going to reach out and touch him, but suddenly there were her fingers on his face, outlining his strong jaw, memorizing the feel of those wondrous cheekbones, experiencing the strength of his heavy black hair, marveling at the feel of his parted lips. She was like a blind person wanting to see with her fingers. But she wasn't blind. She could see the effect of her touch on his incredible face. She was watching a miracle. This man's face was contorted in the agony of his desire—desire for her. His face had become naked for her, hiding nothing. And she became lost, too. No man had ever looked at her with such desire before. No man had ever reached inside her as he was doing, just by looking at her, and grabbed her emotions, turning them over and over, making her open and so in need.

All of the desire so long held in check by the barrenness of her life spoke to her. The long-buried sensuality within her came bubbling forth to the surface of her consciousness. She had been turned off to that part of herself for so long that its emergence frightened her. She was a normal woman, after all. She had not realized that she was still capable of sensuality, of blatantly wanting a man. She had even suspected that her youthful longings for Mr. Right were a cruel joke nature played on adolescent girls—that it was all a myth, that women never really found the fulfillment promised to them in story and song.

But she wanted Jonathan Sky. She wanted to surrender to the desire she saw in his eyes and felt in her own body. She wanted to crawl inside him, to join her body to his, to take a bite of him, anything to merge her flesh with his flesh and her soul with his soul. He made her want to believe that there was fulfillment in this life. He made her want to take the risk and find out.

Beth wished she could tell him what emotions she was feeling just from touching his face. She would like him to know it was all brand-new to her, but she could not speak. Even rational thought was leaving her. She was mesmerized by the moment, by the feelings, by her own aching need.

"Are you going to make love to me?" were the only words she could manage to say. They were whispered and breathless, but Jonathan understood them.

He groaned, and stepping up beside her, engulfed her in his arms. His kiss took away any reservations, any inhibitions, that remained. With his eloquent, demanding lips and tongue, he spoke to her of his need, of what was to follow. She could feel his arousal as their bodies pressed together. Ah, the wonder of that. Appreciation crept into her awareness. It was all right for him to be that way with her. She wanted him to be so. She welcomed his response, and she wasn't repulsed or fearful or frantically searching her mind for a way to postpone what would follow.

But suddenly her chain of thoughts was interrupted by Jonathan's withdrawal of his mouth. No, he couldn't do that, she thought with a gasp. His wondrous mouth had become a part of her. She couldn't give it up.

Then she understood. He was lifting her up in his arms. "Where to?" he said as he carried her into the house and kicked the door shut behind him.

Beth pointed down the hall toward her bedroom, then buried her face against his shoulder. What was happening to her? It was unreal. It was all happening so fast. She was being carried down the hallway past Tricia's room, past the guest room, past the row of Tricia's school pictures in matching silver frames. Jonathan Sky's strong arms were carrying her into her bedroom. He kicked that door shut, also. When he lowered her onto the bed she had shared with her husband, she wondered if she should have directed him elsewhere in the house. Perhaps it was wrong to make love to another man here where she had been with Justin.

She watched Jonathan return to the bedroom door and lock it. He took off his sport coat and threw it over a chair before joining her. Her concern about appropriateness vanished as he began to kiss her mouth like a starving man who had just found fruit.

He consumed her with kisses—deep, possessing kisses. It no longer mattered to Beth where she was as long as she was with this man.

She could not believe the excitement she was feeling. Dizzy, crazy excitement. Jonathan's mouth became the center of her universe. She closed her eyes and gave him her own mouth completely, welcoming his tongue with abandon. Oh, yes. His tongue. It was so sweet, so thrilling. Small murmurs erupted deep from within her—animallike sounds that told him of her need.

Jonathan's hands roamed freely over her body. And she had thought she would never again welcome a man's touch. Well, she had been wrong. Incredibly wrong. Beth was filled with joy at that knowledge. She, who had for years had sex while wearing a nightgown, wanted Jonathan to touch her everywhere. She arched her back in response to his caresses. She longed to rid her body of clothing and offer him her bare flesh. She wanted her skin in contact with his. Would he remove her clothes, or should she? But first he would have to stop kissing her, and she couldn't bear that. How was she going to get undressed? If only she could just will her clothes away. And his. She began tugging at the buttons on his shirt, almost frantic in her need to remove the layers that separated their bodies. Her need filled her body and her mind, making her a different woman—a woman possessed.

She truly wanted him. With her mind and her body, she wanted this man to make love to her, to enter and spill his passion into her. But there was something missing. Something had to be taken care of first. Words needed to be spoken. They couldn't make love without words.

Beth pulled away from him. "No, wait," she gasped. "I have to tell you something."

He looked at her, dazed. "Tell me something?"

Then comprehension showed on his face. And disappointment. "Birth control?" he guessed with a groan.

Birth control? That hadn't even occurred to her, Beth realized with shock. And she was not protected. Justin had had a vasectomy during his first marriage, and Beth had never needed to be concerned with such matters.

But that wasn't what she had wanted to tell him. Beth wanted to let him know the wonder she was feeling. He deserved to know what he, and only he, had done for her unawakened responses. She needed to tell him how incredible it was that she wanted him, really and truly wanted him. Every single part of her wanted him.

She should not have interrupted their lovemaking, however. Beth realized that now. She should have let things flow to their normal conclusion. Jonathan was withdrawing from her. She could tell by the stiffening of his muscles, by the change in his breathing, by the control that had returned to his face.

"You aren't on the pill, I take it," he asked matter-of-factly in his best physician's voice. He could have been talking to a patient.

"No, of course not," Beth said, confused by his instant change from passion to sternness. "Why should I be?"

"So you won't bring unwanted babies into the world to mess up people's lives," he said, his voice hard and uncaring. He pulled away from her arm and sat up.

Beth scrambled to a sitting position and stared at him in horror. He was so cold and distant, this man who just seconds before had been so passionately kissing her and touching her. She didn't understand.

His eyes were black and devoid of emotion, his expression cold as he said, "Next time you want a man to have sex with you, I suggest you come to him prepared."

"But the idea of having sex with you didn't enter my head until a few minutes ago," Beth said, fighting for control. "I'm sorry if you thought otherwise, but how was I supposed to know this was going to happen?"

Jonathan stood and looked down at her. His hair was mussed, and his shirt was wrinkled, its tail hanging out of his jeans.

"This was all a terrible mistake," he said. "I, of all people, should have known better. I'd really like to leave now, but since this is the only chance I'll have for several days to work on your husband's papers, I suppose I'd better take advantage of what precious little time I have. I would appreciate it if you would get me a stiff drink and leave me alone."

"You know where the bar is," Beth said, her voice trembling with hurt and anger. "Get your own drink, and leave *me* alone. And don't forget to shut the bedroom door as you leave."

Chapter Six

The door slammed with a resounding thud. Beth sank back onto the pillow, her breath coming in ragged gasps, her heart beating so furiously in her chest it felt as though it were going to burst. *Am I going to have a heart attack and die like Justin did?* The thought was almost an aside to the inner turmoil she was suffering.

But she was forced to deal first with her physical problem before she could face its cause. She had to control her breathing, her heart, her trembling. And the sexual hunger. It had to be dealt with also. There was to be no relief from that.

Beth rolled over onto her side and wrapped her arms around herself. She drew her knees up to her chest. Slowly her mind and body closed themselves up and slowed themselves down, struggling to control the incredible amount of sexual energy that had been boiling within her.

She lay there for a long time, inert, her only conscious thought to monitor her body's adjustment to the abrupt change in her expectations. She drifted into a sort of stupor, her mind closing down for a while as a protective mechanism, giving her time to garner her physical resources before facing the fact of Jonathan's rejection.

The clock ticked loudly on the bedside table. Caught between the glass and the screen of the window nearest the bed, a fly frantically buzzed. There was a cobweb in the corner above the bureau. Beth made a mental note to bring the broom in here and knock it down.

She drifted along in this detached state for an indeterminate period of time, but eventually the scene between her and the mecurial Dr. Sky began to replay itself in her mind. The temporary reprieve was over. Now there was no way to shut it out. Thoughts of cobwebs and clocks no longer helped. The images unrolled themselves in all their disturbing detail. The passion. The excitement. Mouths seeking. Hands groping. Legs entwined. The hunger. Emotions spiraling ever higher and higher, seeking the ultimate release. And then the beautiful lover turning into an unforgiving monster, the woman left wounded and in pain on her bed.

Beth's emotions assaulted her full force. The impact of what had transpired here on this bed took hold of her. She had crossed over some sort of invisible barrier for the first time in her life and stood ready to give herself to a man totally. There was to be no holding back, no fear, only complete surrender to whatever feelings and emotions awaited her.

And then it had all come down like a castle made of children's building blocks. Devastation. Ruin. Disappointment. She crawled under the rubble, back inside herself. Never again, she vowed. Never again.

"But never again what?" a voice within her taunted. "Never again with this particular man? Never again with any man? The gates to the dam have been opened, lady," the voice harshly informed her, "and you will never be the same again. This man made you *feel*. He showed you what was possible. You could no more go back to what existed before than you could put flooded waters back into the dam."

Beth rolled over and buried her face in the pillow. And she beat the pillow with her fists in silent, angry frustration. She had been given a glimpse of something shiny and glorious, then had it cruelly withdrawn. She didn't know what to do next.

But she had to do something. He was still here, in her house. She couldn't stay a captive in her own bedroom. She absolutely was not going to lie on the bed and cry. She didn't want to grant Jonathan Sky that much power over her—the power to make her cry. No, damn it.

She all but leaped from the bed and grabbed her bathing suit off the hook in the bathroom. She stepped out of her shoes and stripped off the clothing she had so carefully selected earlier in the evening and tossed it on the bed. She dumped her jewelry and watch on the bureau. The pins from her hair followed. She was taking perverse pleasure in dismantling her outfit, her hairdo. The reflection of her naked form in the full-length mirror caught her attention. She approached it slowly, cautiously, her bathing suit hanging from one hand.

This was what Jonathan Sky would have seen had she undressed for him. Standing before her was a slender woman, still young, with breasts full and firm, a smooth belly and long, strong legs. Beth traced the scar from her surgery that ran from her throat to her navel. It had grown faint over the years, no longer the disfiguring angry red slash it once had been. In fact, it was amazing how little it showed. Justin had done a good job. Beth thought of how frail her body looked before that scar, before that surgery. Justin had given her a healthy body. After the operation, he had encouraged her to exercise, exercise, exercise. Much of their courtship involved tennis, racketball, swimming and horseback riding. He had hooked her on physical conditioning. Her body had grown healthy, but through her husband's inadequacies and her own inability to face the problem of their relationship, she had been kept an emotional cripple.

So what was she going to do now? Turn around and get involved with another man who had limited capacity in relationships? Beth asked herself as she wriggled angrily into her bathing suit. Maybe all men who defied the gods by tampering with that sacred organ—the human heart—men who switched hearts from one body to another, who had the power to decide which patient would get a new heart and a new chance at life—maybe all such men by virtue of the incredible responsibility they lived with every day of their lives had to sacrifice their own human emotions in order to survive in the narrow world dictated by their chosen profession. They couldn't be like other people. If they were, they couldn't perform their miracles. It would be too awesome, too frightening, too much responsibility for ordinary people to deal with. Justin had dealt with life-and-death decisions every day. He saw life at its most severe. His profession was the most exacting. His mistakes were the most disastrous. It was as though he gave all his humanity and sensitivity to his patients and became an automaton for the others in his life. His personality seemed to have no room left over for passion, for love, for grief, for pain, but most of all, for imperfections in others. He had to be perfect. How dare those around him be any less.

Were all great surgeons this way? Beth wondered. Was Jonathan Sky going to be such a man? He had been so angry with her because she had not somehow been able to predict the future. He seemed to think she should have known he was going to want to make love to her this evening and should have prepared herself for that eventuality. Her husband had always expected her to be the person he needed her to be. It had never been the other way around. But then she had been very young when she met Justin. She didn't even know what it was she needed in a man. She assumed that any fault in their relationship was hers. Justin had allowed her to think that also, either because he liked her passive and unresponsive or because he, too, assumed any fault must be hers.

A little while ago, Jonathan had instantly assumed the fault was hers for their aborted lovemaking. She wasn't on any sort of birth control.

And how did she respond to his anger?

By apologizing!

She had accepted his blame automatically. What a spineless ninny she was! That was just how she had been with Justin. She had deferred to him in all ways, in all things. She subjugated all her own wants and desires to his. Even when he was wrong, she didn't challenge him, and in not confronting him she had done a grave disservice to them both and to their marriage. Their relationship had gotten stuck in some sort of sick Freudian father-daughter, doctor-patient, master-servant, teacher-pupil relationship, leaving neither one with room to develop a relationship composed of two equals—husband and wife.

Well, she wasn't going to get stuck in that trap again. No way. She would either find a man who understood an egalitarian relationship, or she would forever live alone.

And that meant there could be no Jonathan Sky in her life. What she did not need was another man who made her feel inadequate. And depressed. No way.

Beth suddenly felt better.

She put her hands on her hips and stood with feet apart, looking at her newly determined self in the mirror.

"He really had you going, didn't he?" she asked the reflection. "Didn't know you had it in you, did you, old girl? Maybe there's more inside that scarred chest than you ever gave yourself credit for."

Beth offered the reflection a smart salute and slid open the door onto the patio and headed for the pool. She didn't even break stride when she got to the edge. She simply made the last step a spring and entered the water in a laid-out racing dive.

Lap after lap, she swam. She lost count at thirty-five. Or was it forty-five? It didn't matter. She was in search of exhaustion. Her body would tell her when she got there.

JONATHAN MET LINNEY the summer after his first year of medical training. He had a month off before reporting for year number two.

He had done well in his first year, establishing himself as one of the top students in the class. He was on his way. But life was lonely in California. His undergraduate days at Stanford had not been so bad. The student body was varied, and he had no trouble finding people he felt comfortable with. His class in medical school, however, had been a far more homogenous group, mostly the sons of well-to-do professionals, with an urban background. Jonathan studied most of the time and had not yet developed any close friendships among his classmates.

And back in Oklahoma that summer, more than ever before, he felt the tug of his roots. Having been away for four years of college and a year of medical school, he had put enough distance between himself and Clearwater to forgive some of its shortcomings and to take pleasure in its down-home charm, its creeks and woods, its excellent quail hunting and even better fishing. He enjoyed sitting with the old-timers—both Indian and white—in front of the World War I memorial in the courthouse square and visiting some of his old teachers at the high school. He went to a combination family reunion and powwow and found himself marveling that the Indian heritage of his people had survived, that they could still gather to hear the old stories and songs. He was proud. He found himself with a lump in his throat. Oklahoma was his home. These were his people.

In this positive frame of mind, he even decided to pack up with the cousins and go to the American Indian Exposition in Anadarko, an annual event commonly referred to as the "Indian fair," which brought Indians of all tribes from all over the region for two weeks of pageantry and camaraderie. Most of the visiting Indians lived on the campgrounds. Some came in fancy motor homes, some in beat-up trailers, some in tents. But a large number built brush arbors much like those of their ancestors. Often as not the arbors were equipped with an electric refrigerator hauled from home for the two weeks, and instead of buffalo hides, the occupants slept on cots. But the architecture was authentic.

Traditionally, the Indian fair was a place for the young folks to mingle. The older generations smiled benevolently on the courting and pairing that went on there. They wanted Indian boys and girls to fall in love and marry. If they didn't, one day Indians would disappear and die. Already, most of the purebloods of individual tribes were gone. And the numbers of fullbloods—those who were all Indian but were of mixed tribal origin—were dwindling. Most Indians were like Jonathan—a mixture of Indian and white blood. His father had been half Kiowa and half Delaware. His mother had been half Kiowa and half white. Jonathan had affiliated himself with the Kiowa tribe and had voting rights he had never exercised.

Linney was the elected princess of the Sac and Fox tribe, although she was a quarter Cherokee and a quarter white. Jonathan thought she was the most exquisitely beautiful woman he had ever seen—a romantic vision in white buckskin. Long fringes at the hem and along the sleeves swayed when she walked. The soft buckskin draped provocatively over full breasts and slim hips. Her skin was the color of ripe apricots. Her lashes were the longest Jonathan had ever seen, framing black-brown eyes that singled him out from the minute she saw him.

Linney selected him as her escort for the fair. It was the headiest moment of Jonathan's life, seeming at that moment to top getting a scholarship to Stanford, getting accepted to medical school and even scoring the winning touchdown against Chickasha High

School to propel Clearwater into the state champion-
ship. Linney could have had any young Indian male at
the gathering. She was the newly chosen Miss Indian
Oklahoma. She had been certified the most beautiful
young Indian woman in Oklahoma. Jonathan was
sure she was the most beautiful Indian woman in the
world. She was only seventeen. He had no business
even buying her a Coke. But he was in love, or in
something unlike anything he had ever experienced
before. If he didn't make love to her, he would melt or
evaporate or explode.

For the first week of the fair, he thought of little else
except convincing the luscious Linney to let him make
love to her. Jonathan knew it was all a game, that it
was only a matter of time until she consented. When
he asked her about birth control, however, she appeared insulted. Jonathan thought she was insulted
that he didn't think she was adult enough to manage.
Later, when he brought it up again, he realized that
she was not insulted so much as repulsed by the
thought. Birth control made it all seem planned. Linney wanted the romance and excitement but none of
the responsibility of sex. So Jonathan stopped by the
local drugstore and prepared himself. Soon, he
thought. Please let it be soon.

Not that he wasn't enjoying Linney's little game. It
was the most exciting one he had ever played, and
Linney was a master, playing it out to its fullest, glo-
rying in the power she had over him. She loved his
begging and pleading. She liked saying just how far he
would be allowed to go that evening, giving him a little more leeway each time they were together until she
stopped him with a breathless, anguished, "No,
Johnny. We mustn't. We really mustn't."

Each night he was allowed to conquer just a little bit more of her smooth, brown body—another piece of clothing could be removed, a glimpse of as yet unseen flesh, a new site offered for his hungry mouth.

The last night of the fair, they crawled onto a mattress in the back of a borrowed van, and Linney told him in a heated whisper that tonight was the night, but only if he would pledge undying love and then marriage when she graduated from high school. Even in the height of his passion, Jonathan knew he could not do that. He had no money and no place in his life for a wife. Marriage and family would have to wait.

Linney cried. ''We can't make love unless you promise to marry me,'' she told him tearfully. The tears made her eyes glisten in the moonlight.

Jonathan pleaded for understanding. Surely she didn't want him to make promises he didn't mean. He didn't know when or whom he would marry at this point in his life.

They kissed and argued and touched and argued and took off their clothes and argued some more. Finally, their bodies sought their own mutual solution, and they found themselves joined in fast, violently passionate coupling that satisfied them only momentarily. It wasn't until later that Jonathan remembered the unused contraceptives in his billfold.

In the two weeks before he was scheduled to leave for California, Jonathan spent more time in Vinita than he did in Clearwater. He grew more and more alarmed by Linney's continual talk of marriage, but he was obsessed with their physical relationship. It was with mixed feelings he told her goodbye, promising only to come to see her during Christmas break.

She called him at the end of September to announce her pregnancy. Her father got on the phone and demanded that Jonathan come home at once and do "the honorable thing." He did fly home and almost went through with a hurry-up wedding. His mother tried to talk him out of it.

"Would you want to marry her if she weren't pregnant?" Carlotta Sky asked her eldest child. She stood in the kitchen of their modest home, her hands on her hips. Jonathan carried his dinner dishes from the table and avoided her eyes.

But he eventually admitted to himself and to his mother that no, he wouldn't. He didn't want to marry Linney. Even before summer's end, he had begun to realize that underneath the luscious exterior was a not-very-bright, whining girl-child who was already beginning to bore him.

"Offer child support and go back to California," his mother advised.

But Jonathan couldn't do that. He thought of the unborn child—his child—and agreed to the marriage. It was Linney who called it off, realizing at the last moment that she didn't want to be the wife of a man who had been forced into a marriage.

But Jonathan had never gotten over the guilt.

He had a five-year-old son he had never seen. Linney married the boy she had been going with before she met Jonathan. She told Jonathan's mother that she never wanted to see Jonathan again and that he was to have no contact with the child after it was born. Jonathan's name would not be used on the birth certificate. He would have no legal right to the child.

Jonathan had offered through his mother to give Linney child support, no strings attached. She had refused to accept any money from him until two years ago. Her sister had contacted Jonathan's mother and let her know that child support would no longer be refused if he were still willing to help out. Linney had two more children now. Her husband was out of work, and times were bad for their family.

Jonathan's resident's salary barely supported him at the poverty level, but he sent what he could to Linney and dreamed of the day when he would become a wealthy surgeon. Then he would ask Linney and her husband to allow him to educate the boy and give him a chance to make something of himself—to get away from the stigma of being an Indian in a rural Oklahoma town. Perhaps such beneficence would help him assuage the guilt he still carried over abandoning Linney during her pregnancy. For Jonathan fully realized that with a little encouragement, with a few gentle lies on his part, Linney would have married him gladly. But in spite of his guilt, he was grateful not to be tied down to her. He seriously doubted if he would have been able to stay with three more years of medical school and the years of residency training if he had been responsible for a family. Unlike most of the other physicians in training, he had no financial support from his family. He had gone through undergraduate study and medical school on scholarships and student loans, incurring what seemed like an insurmountable debt. Now he was dedicated to living solely on his meager resident's salary.

He had no money for any sort of social life, and while he had hardly been celibate over the past years, he backed away from a relationship the minute it seemed as if a woman was pushing for marriage. And he was very careful about preventing future pregnancies.

But it wasn't only marriage and children he was avoiding. It was emotional entanglements.

And now, the wall he had carefully erected around his emotions seemed to be crumbling. He felt exposed and vulnerable. And confused. He didn't want to be falling in love.

When he came from the study to the bar to get himself a second brandy, Jonathan saw Beth swimming laps in the pool. He sprawled on the long side of the L-shaped divan and watched her from the darkened room through the floor-to-ceiling windows that overlooked the terrace and pool and the ocean beyond. Quite a layout Dunning had built for himself here, Jonathan noted as he watched the woman swimming. Had the famous surgeon enjoyed it? Did he swim in the pool, entertain in this luxurious living room, take walks on his beachfront? Or had he just built it to make a statement about himself?

And what about her? Did Beth like this home for herself, or was she maintaining it as a tribute to Justin Dunning?

She hadn't been paying tribute to her dead husband earlier in the evening, Jonathan thought wryly. They had come very close to making love—and probably would have if he hadn't come to his senses in time.

But if the birth-control issue had not arisen, neither one of them would have been in any condition to stop the downhill plunge. He had wanted her, Jonathan acknowledged. She was so honest; there had been no deviousness, no game-playing in her responses. When she asked if he was going to make love to her, he almost came unglued. Those eyes looking up at him. Those lips parted, wanting his kiss. He had forgotten what it was like to be that aroused by a woman. Beth really got to him. He felt out of control when he was around her. And that was something he could not allow. He had too much at stake.

Even now, he should be back in the study working instead of sitting here drinking Justin Dunning's excellent brandy and watching the man's wife swim back and forth in his swimming pool. Jonathan was behind in the schedule he had laid out for himself. Yet here he sat, mesmerized, waiting for one view of the whole woman when at last she would emerge from the pool.

Hurry up, pretty lady, he thought, *and finish your swimming so I can get back to work.* He took another sip of the brandy. So fine, the brandy. It was really growing on him. What would it be like, he wondered, always to have the best—to be able to afford the best. The best brandy, the best house, the best wife.

Beth swam with such determination. Up and down the pool, turning in a swift, fluid movement at each end. She had a good stroke, smooth and laid out, with an economy of movement Jonathan admired. He admired everything he had seen of the woman, but he wasn't sure where she was coming from.

Was she a lonely widow just wanting a one-night stand?

He rejected that notion almost at once. But an affair, perhaps.

Or was she wanting another husband?

In a way Jonathan was disappointed that she was no longer the untouchable Widow Dunning. He realized he had romanticized his image of Beth and made an ivory-tower princess out of her. Tonight he had found out that she was a flesh-and-blood woman who had to be dealt with in a down-to-earth fashion. And he didn't know how he felt about that. On the one hand, he wanted to drive to the nearest drug-store and buy birth control protection for himself, then take her back to that bed. On the other hand, he knew he was really going to miss his ivory-tower fantasy lady. Her passing made him sad.

At first, after the disastrous scene in the bedroom tonight, Jonathan had not been able to concentrate on Dunning's papers and journals. But with years of extreme discipline behind him, he knew he could force his mind and his body to do whatever the moment required. He was used to protest, used to muscles saying they were too weary to hold a retractor one instant longer, used to a mind so foggy from lack of sleep that it threatened to shut down, used to the overwhelming emotion involved with life and death threatening to blow all his circuits and shut him down. One learned early in medicine to reach deep inside oneself and find secret reserves that gave the strength, the stamina, the courage, the will, to continue. One learned to put off dealing with personal trauma and tragedy until the job at hand was completed. One did not break down in the operating room.

Jonathan was here in this house to work, here to accomplish a job. What had happened between him and Beth Dunning was dreadful. He suspected he had truly blundered, but he'd deal with that when he had time. In the meantime, he sipped on the brandy to cut the edge of his disappointment and anger before he returned to tackle the job at hand.

The volume of papers waiting to be gone through was overwhelming. Justin Dunning was a man who had made careful journal entries and kept careful files of letters, memos, newspaper clippings, magazine articles, and citations—everything that pertained to his life as a surgeon. It was as though he had a sense that someday someone would be doing just what Jonathan was doing—compiling a picture of his life from the written record. Or perhaps Dunning himself had planned to come back to his carefully kept record in his old age and compile his own tribute. Jonathan sensed that the first sorting of the papers and the first editing of the journal entries had already been done by Dunning himself. Had the heart surgeon thoughtfully chosen what was to be saved and carefully considered what was to be written down? Surely not every letter Dunning had ever received from patients and their families was a grateful one. Had the negative ones that contradicted the carefully cultivated image been thrown away? Jonathan wondered about that. He felt certain that the loved ones of those who had not had dramatic results, or a renewed life, wrote letters too. Yet Jonathan had found no letters that said, "Why did you not just let him die? Why did you put him through all that additional suffering when he was going to die anyway?" Jonathan knew all too well that sometimes death was inevitable and that all the surgeon bought for his patient was more time to suffer.

And the journals seemed to gloss over the surgeries that did not end well. Some outcomes were even omitted. But the successes were there in great detail, along with the verifying letters and newspaper clippings from hometown papers all over the country, showing this or that local citizen returning home with a new heart, with a miracle cure at the hands of the great Justin Dunning.

What Jonathan had seen so far of the written record Justin Dunning had left behind disturbed him. It did not present a truthful picture of the high-risk sub-specialty of cardiovascular surgery. Surgeons who operate on seriously ill people lose patients. That was a given. Dunning had been good. Damned good. He stood at the pinnacle of his field. But he hadn't been a god.

Yet Jonathan realized that he himself had been guilty of elevating the man to superhuman status. All the surgical residents and fellows had. In a way, Jonathan supposed that by doing so they had been on some sort of an ego trip. That such a man had chosen them to train under him made them pretty special, too.

But the larger-than-life persona, Jonathan was beginning to realize, was a carefully cultivated image. Dunning had been very conscious of his supersurgeon image.

Jonathan himself had bought most of the image. He had wanted to hover in the presence of Dunning's greatness, to touch the hem of the master's robe. Dunning had been his hero, pure and simple. But now he was seeing another side to that hero. Dunning had been an egocentric man very intent on building a walk-on-water image for himself. And it served the purposes of those around him to reinforce that image. Dunning was the symbol, the driving force, of Healing Arts. People who had supported Healing Arts with their millions needed for Dunning to be the best in order to prove their own self-worth in electing to support such a worthy man and his cause. And the media enhanced his supersurgeon status. Larger-than-life people made better copy than ordinary folks.

Even Dunning's wife and the dramatic way he had saved her life enhanced the Dunning image, Jonathan realized. Beth had been a seemingly perfect wife for the man—elegant and quietly beautiful but in no way competing with him for the limelight.

Supersurgeon and the ivory-tower princess. Jonathan laughed out loud. Well, the supersurgeon was human, after all, Jonathan was beginning to understand. And the princess was flesh and blood.

It was strange to realize how he had idealized the two. What else had he idealized, Jonathan wondered. What about the practice of medicine? What about surgery? Did he expect too much out of his chosen profession? By becoming an American Indian cardiovascular surgeon, he wasn't going to end world prejudice against minorities. He wasn't going to erase the humiliation his father had suffered. Heart surgery was a worthy and dramatic way to earn a living, but it didn't make him noble or saintly. It wasn't going to take away the pain of his past life. It wasn't going to guarantee him future happiness and a perfect marriage.

He watched an exhausted Beth pull herself from the pool and sit panting on the side, her legs dangling in the water. With her quiet beauty, her innate dignity, her sweet ways, she had touched him more than any woman had in a long time—a very long time. He had wanted to make love to her very much, but something in him had cried out a warning voice. A trap. He was falling into a trap, the warning said. *It's not time to fall in love yet. Don't blow it all now. Don't get involved with a woman—not yet. Don't risk getting an*

*other woman pregnant and complicate your life any
more than it already is.*

Jonathan's life hung in the balance now. He would
either be able to overcome Dr. Christenson's opposi-
tion and be named chief resident, or he would be
forced to settle for less than his goal. Could he be satisfied with "just" being a general or thoracic surgeon
now after setting his sights on the top of the mountain?

An affair with Beth Dunning could not only deter
his energies from his goals; it could also alienate a lot
of important people—people like Martin Morrison—
whose help and support he needed. And if he got her
pregnant . . .

He very easily could have done that tonight. What
a scandal that would cause!

Well, he just wasn't going to think about it anymore. It damned sure wasn't going to happen.

He watched Beth dry herself with a white beach
towel. If only she weren't so lovely, he thought. He
could have made love to her. He stared down at his
hands, remembering how it had felt to touch her. He
still wanted to make love to her.

With the towel over her shoulders shawl fashion, she
entered the house through the kitchen door. Jonathan could hear the door close. He could hear her bare
feet slap on the tile floor of the hallway and sensed
that she was heading for the study in search of him.

He waited in the semidarkness, then heard her steps
approaching the living room. She was pausing on the
top of the three steps that led down into the sunken
living room. She stood there for a long time.

Finally, her voice came across the room. She spoke softly, her tone tinged with sadness, yet the words reached out and surrounded him in the dim room.

"You treated me badly, Jonathan Sky. I didn't plan what happened this evening. As for unwanted pregnancies, it takes two people to make a baby. I had no opportunity to get myself on a birth control program between the time when you first kissed me and we found ourselves on that bed. Some men do take the responsibility for birth control and don't automatically assume it is up to the woman. My husband took care of that in our marriage. I've never used any sort of birth control before—ever."

Jonathan could hear her bare feet slap as she went back down the hall toward her bedroom, the hall he had carried her down during the heights of passion earlier in the evening.

Always before, his future had lain before him in an arrow-straight line. Before Beth.

Now he wasn't so sure.

Chapter Seven

As usual, it was the telephone that awakened Jonathan. Reaching for it, he knocked it to the floor and got twisted up in the cord as he tried to retrieve it in the darkness. The only light in the room was from the telephone's lighted dial.

He had been dreaming of Oklahoma, of Beth, all mixed up together. Part of him was still back there in the dream.

"Yes?" he finally managed to whisper into the mouthpiece.

"Dr. Sky?" the voice inquired.

"Yes."

"This is Nurse Atterbury on Four West."

Nurse Atterbury? Four West? Jonathan felt so groggy—almost drugged. He could not focus his mind. It was the dream. He couldn't return to reality. He mentally replayed what the voice had just said to him. The nurse on Four West was calling him. About a patient, of course. Who was on Four West? Was it the teenager with a congenital heart lesion or the elderly woman with the pacemaker?

"Is it about him or her?" Jonathan mumbled into the phone. No, that didn't make sense. What should he have said?

"I beg your pardon!"

"I mean, which patient are you calling about?" Jonathan said, the puzzled tone in the nurse's voice forcing him into alertness. He listened to the woman's request. A newly admitted patient who couldn't sleep wanted a sleeping pill.

"I get awakened because some guy can't sleep. Somehow that doesn't seem fair," Jonathan said irritably before he gave the nurse permission to administer sleeping medication. "Next time, tell him to count sheep," he said. "Or rock him to sleep."

"Good night, Doctor," Nurse Atterbury said in a carefully neutral tone. The line went dead.

Jonathan fell back on the pillow, stared into the darkness, then uttered a minor oath, dialed the hospital number and asked for Four West. When he heard Nurse Atterbury's voice, he said, "I'm sorry. I was was out of line. You had every right to call me. The sleeping medication should have been written on the patient's orders in the first place."

Now, he thought as he hung up the phone a second time, he could deal with the dream. Beth in Oklahoma. Had he confused her with Linney in his dream?

No, he had replaced Linney with Beth. At first, Beth had been wearing the buckskin dress, until he took it off her. Her hair had been in braids, until he had removed the rawhide ties and unbraided it. But she wasn't Indian. She was definitely the fair-skinned, wavy-haired woman he had been with earlier in the evening, the woman he had almost made love to in the luxurious bedroom she had once shared with her husband.

Jonathan desperately tried to force himself back into the dream. There had been tom-toms beating and singing in the distance—over there by the grandstand. They were at the Indian fair in Anadarko, where he had met Linney, where the son he had never seen was conceived. But the dream did not deal with Linney or his illegitimate child. It dealt only with him making love to Beth in the world of his youth, in the world in which his roots went deep and strong. Her skin was alabaster in the moonlight. Her hair was silky and fine in his hands. They were making love on a blanket spread out in the middle of a grove of trees. Gentle breezes caressed their moist nude skin. He was stretched out on his back, and Beth was kneeling astride his middle, her hands pressed against his chest, her hair falling in a curtain about her face. His hands wandered from her hair to her breasts as she began a slow, rocking movement that moved him even deeper within her. She pushed hard against his chest, arching her back. Small animal sounds rushed from her lips. She was fantastic.

As much as he loved watching her, feeling her breasts, he wanted to feel the length of her body under him. He had to feel that, to feel his body moving in hers. He pulled her face down, and their lips touched, softly at first, nibbling, feather-light kisses that became more and more demanding. He plunged his tongue between her open, waiting lips.

Oh, yes. The sweetness of her made him drunk.

Her breasts pressed against his chest—flesh on flesh, erotic beyond belief.

With a swift movement, he rolled both of them over. Now she was beneath him, her legs wrapped around his waist. They were locked together as though they had been made that way. It was glorious. Absolutely glorious.

It would have been perfect if it had been real. Perfect.

But Jonathan knew as the images played themselves on the screen of his mind that they weren't real. They were made up. It wasn't even a real dream. He was half awake, continuing his dream with a manufactured fantasy. He had been robbed of the semireality offered by his dream when the damned telephone rang. And the fantasy was only serving to frustrate him. He elected to back away from it.

He switched on the lamp, then opened his eyes and stared at the ceiling. A gray stain in the shape of the state of Texas spread itself on the plaster surface, the telltale evidence of an overflowed bathtub in the room above his.

Where would his sleeping mind have taken him, Jonathan wondered as he mentally located Dallas and Houston on the stain. He recalled a song that claimed a dream was a wish your heart made when you're fast asleep. Was his mind wishing only that he could love the elegant and beautiful Beth, or was it addressing a deep-seated need that he love her on his home turf and not in the bed she had shared with the late, great Justin Dunning her husband and his mentor? But why not a dream that had them making love here in his small resident's quarters or at a neutral site such as a hotel or the beach. Why had his dream transported them to Oklahoma? To the Indian fair, of all places?

Perhaps the dream represented deep-seated wistfulness. Perhaps a part of him understood. It was erasing the painful memory of Linney from his mind and replacing her with Beth. It would have been Beth he made pregnant.

But then it would have been Beth he offered to marry, Beth and their baby for whom he would have offered to give up his educational goals. Maybe Beth would not have refused him. He would have had to get a job teaching school or working in a bank. Or maybe he would have ended up painting gaudy colors on cheap souvenirs for the tourists. Maybe it was just a crazy guilt of a dream with no sense to be made of it at all. He didn't know Beth back in his Oklahoma days. But he knew her now. And now he was already a physician—a thoracic surgeon. He'd never teach school in Clearwater, Oklahoma. He was on the verge of reaching his academic and personal goals. And even if he didn't get the fellowship in cardiovascular surgery, he could still enter practice as a chest surgeon. He wondered if any other American Indian had ever completed his training in thoracic surgery. He might be the first. He had proved himself. It didn't mean as much as he once thought it would, but he had shown that the son of Billy Joe Sky, an Indian from Clearwater, Oklahoma, could go far. If he didn't get the cardiovascular fellowship, it would not change that. Getting involved with a woman now wouldn't take away what he had already accomplished.

But Beth wasn't just a woman. She was the wealthy widow of Justin Dunning. Marriage to her could mean not only having the man's wife but moving into Dunning's house, sleeping in his bed. Jonathan wondered if that was a factor in Beth's mystique, if a part of himself wanted to be the next Dunning in every way, including marrying the man's wife and living in his house. Yet realistically Jonathan knew he never could live in that house. Never. And Beth? Could he live with her? He didn't know. If Beth had been the widow of some anonymous man, would Jonathan still feel this incredibly complex battle within himself that one time lined up the facts on one side of the battle line, then switched them around and lined them up on the other?

Jonathan realized he was perspiring and kicked the covers off. He lay there for a time in the stuffy room, then finally got up and opened a window. He turned off the light and sprawled back across the bed, lying on his belly.

A refreshing breeze cooled his moist skin. It felt good. But he knew it wouldn't make him sleep. He was too caught up in thoughts of her.

Why was he so concerned about analyzing his attraction to Beth Dunning, Jonathan thought irritably. It didn't really matter one way or the other why. She would never have anything to do with him now, Jonathan realized. He had really screwed things up with her. She would never risk having any sort of relationship with him, not after what had happened.

Talk about overreacting! Lecturing her on birth control! Damn, what a jerk he had been, when all the time he had wanted her so desperately. But then his desire had been mixed with animosity over who she was and the kind of house she lived in and his own reluctance to become entangled. Maybe he had picked the birth control issue just to get him out of hot water. He could have taken time out to go to the drugstore for some sort of protection. Or they simply could have enjoyed each other's bodies without consummating their desire. He would have found a way to please her.

"Stop it!" Jonathan said out loud. "Quit thinking about what you could have done. Cut out the self-torture."

But his fantasy went on, wrapping itself around his mind, taking control of his body and playing itself out to completion. Embracing a pillow as a substitute for the woman he wished were in his arms, he fell asleep.

"But can't you see what bad publicity it would be if it becomes known that Justin Dunning left his wife and daughter penniless?" Martin Morrison complained. "You're just going to have to hold on at least a while longer—until we get the funding secured for the rest of the hospital expansion."

The snowy-haired hospital administrator got up and started pacing the floor in front of his desk, his agitation apparent. Beth's plight meant nothing to him except that it might somehow damage the image of the foundation's legendary founder.

Beth sighed with exasperation. "And just how am I supposed to hold on? It will become public knowledge when that house is sold for past taxes or when one of our California fires burns it up and I can't rebuild it because I had to let my insurance on the place lapse. I have no money, Martin. Justin's will prohibits me from selling the house, but his estate provides no money for its upkeep. I work like a slave all day trying to maintain the place. Have you any idea how much money and effort it takes to keep up a house like that? I alone am now doing what a housekeeper, a gardener and a pool-maintenance company used to do. After Justin died, I thought perhaps I would try to go back to school and prepare myself for some sort of career, but I can't afford the luxury of doing that. I'd get a job, but I'm afraid whatever I'd earn would only be a drop in the bucket, and I don't have time to work away from home when my every waking hour seems to go into keeping the house and grounds up. I don't dare let the place deteriorate, because renting it for enough to cover the mortgage payments, taxes and upkeep is the only solution I can see. If the house is sold for taxes, Tricia will inherit nothing from her father. Justin had borrowed against his insurance, borrowed against future earnings—and most of it went to the foundation. We had no investments, no savings.''

"What about the book project?" Martin said, pausing in his pacing and mussing his carefully styled hair in an uncharacteristic gesture. "How are you and Dr. Sky doing with that? Perhaps you can prepare a proposal and sell the idea to a publisher. I really need you to hang on at least until the end of the year, Beth. We just can't afford any detrimental publicity."

"Martin, you aren't listening to me. I owe a hell of a lot of money for back taxes on that house. I don't have next month's mortgage payment. Tricia and I are very close to being put out on the street," Beth said in exasperation. "I'm almost broke. Every small expense takes on the dimensions of a catastrophe—Tricia's prom dress, a visit to the dentist, a broken pool pump, a dead tree that needs to be cut down before it falls over on the roof of my uninsured house. I've got to rent the house. I have no choice. Tricia is against it, but we'll have to move into an apartment—a cheap apartment. We simply can't afford that house.''

"What about the book?" Martin repeated pointedly, staring down at her. "I haven't heard you mention anything about it or Dr. Sky."

"That isn't working out very well," Beth told him, avoiding his gaze by staring out the window. Her heart accelerated its beat just at the mention of Jonathan's name, Beth realized with irritation.

"I'm not sure the book was such a good idea in the first place," Beth said. "And it will be so long before any actual money is realized from it that it won't help my short-term plight. Since I can't afford to go back to school and finish a degree, then I need to find work, Martin. I really need to get on with my life. And the book—well, maybe it was just a way of hanging on to the old life a while longer and avoiding the inevitable. It was only going to be a short-term solution at best."

"I'm not sure I understand you, Beth," Martin said, rocking back and forth on the heels of his aligator shoes. "You were married to one of the greatest heart surgeons who has ever lived. How could you not be willing to cooperate in this project, to see that his papers are properly saved for study and contemplation by future generations and to see that his memory is preserved in book form? Justin deserves that, Beth, and you owe him. This foundation and its hospital are the living embodiment of Justin Dunning. As they grow and prosper and contribute to mankind, so will the endowment left to us by him continue to grow and prosper and benefit. You and I both, more than anyone else, have the responsibility to see that Justin's dreams are brought to fruition. I just don't see how you as his widow can possibly feel otherwise, Beth. To do so is to deny Justin and everything he stood for."

"Stop it, Martin! Can't you ever talk about anything except the foundation and Justin!" Beth said much too loudly, resisting the urge to put her hands over her ears. "I'm tired of it—sick to death of it. I have lived with my 'responsibility' to Justin for the past ten years. I served him well. You know that. I did everything possible to take every burden from his shoulders so he could concentrate solely on medicine and the foundation. But Justin is dead. He has been for a year. When does my responsibility to Justin end and my responsibility to myself begin? When? Please tell me."

"You surprise me, Beth," Martin said in a paternalistic voice that Beth found extremely annoying. "I would think you'd realize that in a sense your responsibility to Justin's memory never ends. As his widow, you will always be a reflection of him. But certainly after we get this wing funded and built, the situation will ease, and you can do what you need to do about the house. And then if you have to seek employment, it would not be quite so damaging. But in the meantime I need for you and Dr. Sky to show the Wisharts that we're making some headway on the literary project. I thought it would be nice if we invited them out to your home and showed them the journals and mementos that will be used in the Dunning Collection of the Library. And you know how thrilled the Wisharts are about the book. They want to talk to publishers about it. Mr. Wishart indicated he has some connections in the publishing industry that might be helpful not only in getting it published but in getting it promoted. I was thinking about Sunday evening. Just cocktails and hors d'oeuvres by the pool would be nice. I've already told Dr. Sky he should plan to attend."

Martin returned to his desk. He regarded Beth from his oversized leather chair. "As for your financial picture, I'll give Justin's attorney a call. Perhaps it's just a case where better management on your part might solve the problem. But if I am given proof that things are really as grim as you say, then I can arrange for some sort of retainer from the foundation in return for your fund-raising activities. Such an arrangement would have to be kept very private, and you would, of course, be expected to maintain an above-reproach image as the widow of Justin Dunning."

As Beth left Dr. Morrison's office and headed for the parking garage, she experienced a sick feeling of defeat. She was trapped. Of course, she couldn't do anything to damage the medical-center expansion project, and she did need financial assistance at least until the book was published. She'd have to keep Justin's image untarnished for a while longer, and she would have to cooperate with the continued cataloging of his papers and the organization of the book. Martin was right about that. But damn it, was he right about the other things he said? Did her responsibility to her dead husband follow her to her own grave?

Beth wound her navy-blue Cadillac down the spiral ramp toward the highway exit. It was a wonderful car with a fantastic stereo system, but maybe she could sell the Cadillac and buy an economy car. She had always felt rather ostentatious in the expensive automobile, anyway. Justin had driven a Mercedes that Beth had already sold.

She tried to think of other moneymaking strategies on the drive home, but a song on the radio about "looking for love in all the wrong places" forced her finally to deal with the fact that she would be seeing Jonathan again in the near future.

It had been two weeks since their ill-fated evening together. Beth had arranged to be out of the house on the two subsequent times he was scheduled to come work on the book project. Tricia looked only slightly puzzled at the time.

"I have a meeting at the hospital," Beth explained. "Just let him in and offer him a cup of coffee. Tell him I won't be here but to leave me a note about his progress and anything I need to type."

The second time—a Sunday evening—Tricia asked why the only times that Beth went out were the evenings Dr. Sky came to the house. Beth offered a lame explanation about another meeting, which she knew Tricia doubted. She wasn't sure what she would tell her stepdaughter next Wednesday night before she left the house. Maybe she would simply be honest and say, "I don't like the man."

And that would be only partially honest. Beth didn't like Jonathan Sky. But she was affected by him. Hardly an hour went by that she didn't find herself reliving some part of that scene in her bedroom.

It had been within a very short time the best and the worst of her sexual experience.

With Jonathan Sky as her guide, Beth had turned a corner and come face-to-face with the extent of her own sexuality, something that—odd as it might seem for a woman who had been married for nine years and widowed for one—had not happened to her before.

Beth had accepted sex as her marital duty and kept it in a compartment carefully walled away where she wouldn't have to deal with it except for the infrequent times when Justin expected what he would have regarded as his "husbandly rights." There had been occasions when Beth took pleasure in satisfying her husband, although she enjoyed no fulfillment herself. And before marriage there had been Philip the Frenchman, and a few mysterious adolescent crushes on a few gangling youths during her school days in Switzerland that made her feel all flushed and restless. There had even been a few adult crushes in the years since her marriage that had threatened to awaken some dormant force within her and served to alert her to the fact that her marriage was inadequate. But she had banished such thoughts from her awareness. There was no place for them in her life. Inadequate or not, she was in a marriage that she felt obligated to preserve—and besides, the thoughts frightened her. She was better off without them.

But now she wasn't married. She wasn't an adolescent. The dormant drives were still there. From time to time she had half dreamed of finding physical fulfillment with a man, but she assumed that sexual fulfillment and falling in love would occur simultaneously. She had not been in love with her husband, not in the romantic sense.

But she wasn't in love with Dr. Sky, either. She might have thought she was falling in love with him before he treated her so shabbily. But now she knew she couldn't possibly love him. Yet she still thought of his hands on her body. She still remembered how desperately she had wanted to be naked with him, to have their flesh touching. And yes, she had actually felt her body opening up to his, delivering its own not-too-subtle message to her brain. Her body had been ready and waiting for sex. That didn't seem fair. She had never experienced such physical attraction before. It had nothing to do with love. How could her body be so stupid? And why did the yearnings continue to plague her? It was over. It had been over before it began.

TRICIA DUNNING had worshiped her father. They had never had a close father-daughter relationship, but she was terribly proud to be his daughter and had always been pitifully appreciative of any gesture of affection he offered her.

What memories she had of her mother were of a quiet woman who took her to the beach often and sat looking out to sea by the hour while Tricia made sand castles, complete with moats, using a set of empty cans and discarded plastic containers as her molds.

"Look, Mother," Tricia would call, eager to show off her engineering marvels.

Felicia Dunning would look vacantly at her daughter's creations, smile her vague, sweet smile and return to an endless vigil.

Tricia used to wonder what her mother was looking for out there on the horizon. Sometimes she would sit with her and watch, hoping that the object of her mother's perpetual vigil would appear. But other than an occasional passing ship far out to sea or fishing boats closer in, there was nothing out there but endless water.

Justin was often at the hospital in the evenings, and toward the end of her life, Felicia had taken to tucking her daughter in bed for the night and leaving her in the house with the housekeeper. Felicia would then return to the beach. Tricia would get up sometimes and creep to the edge of the terrace. She could see her

mother down there, her slim form made ethereal by
the luminous quality of moonlight on pale sand.
Alone. Always alone by the water's edge.

One night Justin came home to a sleeping Tricia,
but Felicia was no place to be found. She had vanished. Tricia's last memory of her mother was a soft
good-night kiss planted on her cheek and a whisper.
"I'm going for a quick swim in the ocean. You go on
to sleep. I love you more than anything."

Her sandals and jacket were found on the beach the
next morning. No one ever saw Felicia again. The
court decided eventually that she drowned and was
washed out to sea. Justin had a funeral and erected a
tombstone. Tricia cried for her mother at night and
had nightmares for a year and a half after her mother's death. Finally, however, Beth came. At first, six-
year-old Tricia resisted Beth's overtures of care and
affection, but eventually the lonely girl grew to accept and then to love her new stepmother. Once love
set in, however, Tricia could not bear to let Beth out
of her sight. And she grew hysterical at the notion of
Beth's going down to the beach.

Gradually, however, Tricia's fears abated some-
what, and she grew into a pretty, well-adjusted teenager. Her father's death, however, brought back the
old fears of abandonment. What if Beth married
someone else? Would a new husband want Beth's
stepdaughter. And Beth talked of their leaving the
house and living elsewhere. Tricia would be without
home or family.

The old nightmares began to return.

"I'm here, honey," Beth would say gently, strok-
ing Tricia's hair to calm her, bringing her cups of
warm milk, just as she had done when Tricia was six—

and in the same blue mug with a unicorn on its side. Beth would stretch out beside her on the bed and talk of plans for the next weekend, of what they could cook when Tricia's grandmother came to dinner.

But Tricia was afraid.

Tricia wasn't sure just what had happened between her stepmother and the tall, reserved resident surgeon with the dark eyes and look of quiet strength, but she was old enough and wise enough to realize that Beth's sudden desire to be out of the house when Dr. Sky arrived was probably the result of a quarrel. Had it been a lover's quarrel? Tricia was near enough to womanhood to sense that was the case. Tricia could think of no other reason for Beth to be so uncomfortable in the man's presence. Her stepmother even felt the need to leave her own home while Jonathan Sky was there working on her father's papers. If the young doctor had been a wicked man, Beth would not have gone off and left a teenage girl in the house with him. Obviously he was trustworthy. But Beth was so disturbed by his presence that she ran from it.

Jonathan Sky wanted to become a heart surgeon like her father. If he and Beth patched up their differences, was he planning to take over for her father in Beth's life, Tricia wondered.

And if he does, what will happen to me? Tricia asked herself.

As Tricia helped Beth with the preparations for Sunday evening, she knew without asking that Dr. Sky would be among the "few people" who were coming over for cocktails. Why else would Beth be so nervous and distracted. She spilled a jar of pickles on the kitchen floor and fretted all afternoon about the house smelling of pickle juice. She twice rearranged the buffet table by the pool before threatening storm clouds forced her to move everything into the dining room. And she snapped at Tricia for forgetting to run the vacuum cleaner.

"Good grief, Tricia. Do I have to do everything around here? I'd think you'd be a little more responsible."

Beth apologized almost as soon as the words were out of her mouth, but Tricia felt a cold knot of fear take hold of her heart. Her first mother had been taken away by a vast, uncaring ocean. Was this one being taken away from her by the mysterious Indian surgeon with the unfathomable eyes?

Tricia had never seen Beth so nervous. As the day wore on, her stepmother seemed like a frantic butterfly with no place to light. She went on to the next task without completing the previous one. She decided at four o'clock that she had to clean the oven even though it ruined the nails she had just manicured.

When Tricia went into Beth's bedroom that evening, she found her mother close to tears over a spot that hadn't come out of the dress she picked up from the cleaners the day before and planned to wear that evening. Tricia stood by coldly without offering any advice. She recalled times in the past when she sat on the bed and watched her stepmother dress for the evening—when she had been entertaining at home or going out with her father. Beth had never been so concerned about what to wear for her husband.

The pair of evening pajamas Beth pulled out of the back of the closet were very becoming, Tricia had to admit. The white crepe looked smashing against her stepmother's tan skin and dark hair. The silver dangling earrings looked glamorous. Her slim waist was accentuated by a colorful belt. Beth was beautiful. This made Tricia both proud and worried. How could Dr. Sky help but love her?

And Tricia already knew what Beth herself refused to acknowledge—that Beth was in love with Jonathan Sky.

Chapter Eight

When the doorbell rang, Beth jumped, then turned to look and see if Tricia had noticed her reaction. Tricia continued arranging canapés on a tray and seemed not to notice Beth's nervousness.

"I'll get it," Beth said needlessly, and hurried down the hall, her heart racing. It was a few minutes before six o'clock. Ordinarily she would assume that Jonathan was going to be late. Physicians were always late. But she knew it was he before she opened the door.

"I wanted to arrive before the others," he said as he stepped in the door. "I have something for you."

He held out a long, narrow package to her and watched as she unrolled the paper from the slender object.

It was a clay pipe beautifully painted with distinctly Indian patterns and decorated with a tuft of gray-and-brown feathers fastened to the stem with a rawhide thong. Beth looked at him questioningly.

"It's a peace pipe," he said, his gaze on her face, his hand reaching out to touch her arm. But his hand never made contact. He looked past her to the wall of windows and the swimming pool, to the row of palms dancing in the gusting wind of an approaching storm, to the churning ocean and the cloud-laden sky. His gaze returned to the luxurious room, taking in its Oriental rugs, the huge Russell oil of the painted desert that hung over the fireplace, the elegant furnishings, the cathedral ceiling with its heavy beams. His expression hardened. His hand returned to his side. "It's still hard for me to believe people live in houses like this," he said.

Then he looked down at the peace pipe in her hand. "My dad made those for tourists. That's how he supported us. Our whole house would have fit in your living room."

Beth didn't know how to respond. Was the pipe a gesture of peace? At first, she thought it was, but now he seemed so antagonistic, not at all like someone who was making peaceful overtures.

"It's very nice," Beth said, fingering the delicate clay stem of the pipe. "Thank you."

Jonathan glanced back at her face. "You look beautiful," he said, his words sounding like an accusation. "No, strike that. You *are* beautiful. I brought the pipe to break the ice and give me some way to begin to make things right with you. I'm not sure if that's possible or even what 'making it right' means. I just feel bad about what happened between us. You didn't deserve that. I shouldn't take my problems out on other people."

Beth didn't know how to respond, so she didn't say anything. She placed the pipe beside a vase on one of the two glass-and-chrome étagères that stood side by side in the hallway and crumpled the wrapping paper in her hands. She felt terribly self-conscious as Jonathan followed her into the living room. She disposed of the wrapping paper in the wastebasket behind the bar.

"I've mixed whiskey sours, or I'd be glad to fix you something else," she said. Her voice sounded funny to her. She picked up a glass and realized she was trembling. She put the glass back down again.

Jonathan didn't say anything but stood across the bar looking at her. Beth felt helpless and lost as she looked into those intense dark eyes. Inexplicable tears stung at her own eyes. The memory of the pain and humiliation he had caused her came flooding back. But even so, she wanted him still.

She drank in his unique beauty. Everything about him fascinated and aroused her. Everything. The line of his jaw. The curve of his mouth. The arch of his brows. The two vertical creases in his forehead between his eyes. The intensity of those dark eyes. The thick blackness of his heavy hair. The obvious strength of his athlete's body. The sight of him made her ache. His appearance characterized the man himself—strong, different, brooding, a force to be reckoned with.

She wanted to know the rest of him as she had come to know his face. She wanted to see the arms, the shoulders, the chest, the thighs, the manhood that was covered by those clothes. She wanted to know him, to memorize him, to crawl inside him.

"I have an illegitimate son back in Oklahoma," he was saying. "It's a source of great pain for me and a mistake I don't wish to repeat. I know nothing can excuse how I acted, but I hope that by knowing this you can understand my behaviour at least a little. I wouldn't blame you if you hated me, but I find it matters to me a great deal what you think of me. I don't know what is going on in my mind. I can't get involved with you or anyone else. I am, if anything, single-minded of purpose and unrelentingly ambitious. I have no time for romance. No money for courting a woman. My dating you would cause big problems at the hospital at a time when I can ill afford to alienate anyone. If I got involved with you, it would take my mind off my work, ruin my chances to become chief resident, screw up the cardiology fellowship. It's impossible. Out of the question. You're the one woman in the world I absolutely can't become involved with. But I want you so much it's becoming an obsession. It *is* an obsession. I..."

His voice trailed off. His hand reached out again as though to touch her cheek, but he withdrew it. They stood across the bar from one another, staring at each other, their gazes locked, their bodies tense.

She was riveted by his eyes, yet the rest of her body seemed to be spinning around and around like an Alice tumbling, falling, floating, helplessly down the endless hole into a waiting Wonderland. She parted her lips to speak but found she had no words.

The weakness infusing itself into her legs threatened to buckle her knees, and she was barely conscious of grabbing the counter's edge for support. She could feel her insides churning, rearranging themselves, preparing themselves as desire coursed through every vein, every nerve.

A force field manifested itself between their bodies. Like the atmosphere before a hurricane strikes, the air was heavy, laden with electricity, ominous. There was no escape. Jonathan felt it, too. She could see it in his eyes, in the way he looked at her, in the way his muscles tensed and his jaw clenched.

Beth was beyond logic, beyond fear. A decision was not necessary. Jonathan didn't need to make one. She didn't need to make one. It had been made for them. They could no more prevent what was going to happen to them than they could prevent the approaching storm from coming. Like a ferocious hurricane, the winds of desire would sweep over them, catching them up, having their way with them. They were helpless to resist. Mutely, they acknowledged inevitability.

They were standing but a few feet apart, their gazes locked, when Tricia came into the room.

Tricia eyed Jonathan warily, offering him only the most perfunctory of greetings. "I'm off to Kimmie's," she told her mother. "See you in the morning. Have a nice party."

When the front door slammed behind Tricia, Beth said, "She's spending the night with a friend."

Jonathan let out a small moan and trailed his fingertips down her cheek. "You know I want you?" he asked softly.

"Yes," she acknowledged, and leaned into his caress. Beth closed her eyes to block out all other sensation but that of his fingers on her face. He would kiss her soon. She wanted that very much.

But the sound of the door chime prevented the anticipated kiss. Beth opened her eyes.

"Later," he promised as his lips brushed her forehead.

As the others began to arrive, Beth became two women. Outwardly, she went through the motions of being hostess, seemingly calm, competent, making small talk over drinks, managing beautifully. But that woman was on automatic pilot, scarcely aware of what she was doing but carrying it off because similar duties had been performed often enough in the past to have been programmed into her brain. Inwardly, she was awash with desire. The inward woman was alive and feeling at an incredibly high level. The presence of Jonathan Sky was more potent than all the liquor lined up on the glass shelves behind the bar, more potent that anything Beth had ever experienced before. She caught a glimpse of herself in the mirrored wall behind the shelves of glasses. The anticipation of what was to come manifested itself in the heightened color of her cheeks and the vivacious sparkle in her eyes. She smiled at herself, then laughed. Martin came up behind her and quietly cautioned her not to drink so much.

Her eyes widened in surprise, and she smiled. "But Martin, I haven't touched a drop." And she hadn't. But his words served as a warning. She forced her outward self back into the cool, calm mode that was expected of her.

She circulated through the room, refilling drinks, visiting with her guests and stealing glances at Jonathan.

"It's hard to believe he's been gone for one whole year," Jacob Wishart said, an arm resting solicitously around her shoulders. "I know it's been a hard year for you, my dear."

"Yes, it has," Beth said sincerely. "Tricia and I miss him very much." And she meant it. It would have been easy to bury herself figuratively along with Justin. In a way, the people assembled here in her living room expected it of her. Martin, the Wisharts, the foundation board members, their wives. Before, she would have felt drawn into their cause, compelled to make the sort of sacrifice they expected of her, to remain the shadowed wife forever.

But that was before she met Jonathan. He brought the winds of change into her life. He forced her to think of matters other than her day-to-day life. His attention made her believe in herself, and that she could be a real person.

Even if their relationship turned out to be a disaster, Beth realized Jonathan Sky had given her a very precious gift. He had given her herself. She was a flesh-and-blood woman who didn't want to be buried in the past along with her dead husband. She had a future. That was frightening but wonderfully exciting. In fact, she felt more alive tonight than she had ever been in her life—not just because she was going to make love with Jonathan for the first time, with the only man she had ever truly desired, but because she felt a new life was out there waiting for her. She was standing in chapter one of that new life. The pages were empty and waiting to be filled. She didn't know what words would be written. All she knew was that she didn't want to live the rest of her life shut up in the closed book of Justin's life. She wanted her own book, her own life.

"For God's sake, Beth, look like a widow," Martin whispered angrily. "You act like a teenager heading for the prom."

"Really?" she whispered back. "I never went to a prom when I was a teenager. Maybe I'm a late bloomer."

Martin gave her an accusing look and took the glass she was holding from her hand. He put it to his nose and smelled it. Then he took a sip. Beth laughed at the incredulous look on his face.

"What's the matter, Martin. Don't you like ginger ale?"

"Are you high on something?" he asked out of the corner of his mouth.

She looked him in the eye. "Yes, I am. I'm high on life."

"I don't know what's gotten into you, Beth," he said, his voice stern and paternalistic, "but please try and remember your responsibility. We save lives at that Healing Arts. We need money to keep on doing that. And this fund-raising drive needs you to speak for Justin, to tell of his dreams for the future of Healing Arts. No one else saying those words can have the impact that you do. You realize that, don't you, Beth?"

She stared at the fleshy but still handsome face of her husband's most dedicated supporter. There was an arrogant lift to his eyebrows she had never noticed before. Suddenly, in spite of his domineering attitude toward her, the man seemed pitiful to Beth. How sad to live one's life through another. Beth understood that now. And now that Justin was gone, Martin Morrison invested his energies and ambitions in Healing Arts.

He was waiting for her answer. She composed her face to look more widowlike and said, "Yes, I realize I speak for Justin. I wonder when I get to speak for myself."

Beth halfheartedly returned her attention to Betty Wishart. As the woman droned on, Beth nodded her head when appropriate and murmured agreeable sounds at the correct times. Yes, Justin had been a man among men. Yes, he would long be remembered. She maintained a calm, poised exterior, but inside, Beth still was spinning, spiraling, falling down the magic well. She and Jonathan would endure the evening. At its end they would be alone. That was all she knew. She would worry about what came after later.

One by one the board members began to take their leave until at last only the Wisharts, Martin and Jonathan remained. Beth was aware that Martin was negotiating dinner plans with the Wisharts. She didn't want dinner. She just wanted to be alone with the man whose eyes had never left her all evening, with the man who she knew was feeling exactly the same yearnings that she herself was experiencing.

But oddly she found she really didn't mind putting off the moment when they would be alone. The anticipation was its own wonderfully agonizing game. She would sit at a table with Jonathan and the others, eating her meal, aware of what he was thinking, knowing that they would eventually be alone.

They went to the Greenhouse, a spectacular garden restaurant built under a full acre of glass. They were seated in a white wicker gazebo surrounded by hanging plants and potted fig trees. The trees twinkled with hundreds of tiny white lights. It was a fairyland.

Beth's lobster was fantastic. Nothing had ever tasted so fine. The wine was full and dry. The chocolate mousse was sinfully rich. The after-dinner coffee had never been so satisfying. Her gaze and Jonathan's would meet, linger for a knowing, intimate glance, then pass on, only to return a minute later. It was a wonderfully erotic game. Their secret. Soon they would be in each other's arms. Soon they would taste and feel each other. They would be one. Heaven awaited them, they told each other with their eyes.

Throughout the meal, the talk of fund-raising—benefit galas, art auctions and craft fairs, continued. Betty Wishart was enthusiastic. She eagerly thought of ways she could help.

"The Cynthia Wishart Memorial Research Wing is so important to Jacob and me," Betty Wishart confided to Beth across their corner of the table. "It's how we keep the memory of our little girl alive. It's the most important thing in my life, but then, I'm sure you understand how important it is for those of us left behind to memorialize our loved ones."

Beth frantically thought of some way to change the subject. She didn't want to hear any more of Betty's platitudes. She looked up gratefully as the waiter refilled her coffee cup.

"The coffee is so good here," Beth said as she picked up her cup. "I wonder what kind they use."

Betty did not respond to her comment. She waved the waiter away from her own empty cup and continued with the one-sided conversation. "Martin speaks of you so glowingly, my dear. He's told us what a good wife you were and how you are determined to see that your husband's dream lives on. I admire you so much. And I want you to know that Jacob and I intend to take a back seat to you at all these fund-raising events. You're the one people want to talk to, to tell how he saved their life or the life of a loved one, or prolonged it, as he did with our little Cynthia. You're the closest thing we have left to Justin. That's quite a responsibility for a young woman, but Martin tells us that you are quite capable and willing to fulfill it."

Beth stared down at the woman's hand as it solicitously patted her arm. She wanted to tell Mrs. Wishart that she wasn't capable and willing, that she wasn't the selfless widow that Martin had made her out to be. But she felt trapped. The cause was bigger than she.

"Do you feel all right, my dear," Mrs. Wishart asked kindly.

"Yes, I'm fine," Beth said, realizing a headache was pushing against her temples. She didn't want a headache. She wanted Jonathan. She looked at him, her eyes beseeching.

"I'm scrubbing on the first case in the morning," Jonathan said, pushing back his chair. "I'm sorry to break up this lovely gathering, but I really must go. Mrs. Dunning, may I give you a ride home?"

Beth nodded and pushed her own chair back. But before she could offer their good-nights, Martin put a firm, restraining hand on her arm. "Nonsense, Jonathan, my boy. Beth's house is completely out of your way. I'll drop her off."

Beth watched helplessly as Jonathan shook hands around the table and thanked the Wisharts for including him in the dinner. When he came to Beth's hand, he lingered just a fraction of a second longer than necessary. Her heart jumped a beat.

Martin noticed. He cleared his throat pointedly.

The hospital administrator lectured her on the way home. He was shocked and disappointed. Beth must be above gossip. She absolutely must not get involved with one of her husband's residents. Like it or not, the script that had been written for her had placed her only about one rung down the ladder from the Madonna.

"I'm not cut out to be a saint," Beth protested.

"Don't knock sainthood," Martin said firmly. "Have you really stopped to assess what the Dunning name means to you, how much you have traded off it in the years since you married Justin? Don't pull a Jacqueline Kennedy and heedlessly throw away the deference and honor that being the widow of a legend brings. And if you don't care enough about yourself, think of Dr. Sky. If you enter into a ...ah, relationship with him, it could very well jeopardize his appointment as chief resident and the granting of his fellowship the following year—his whole career.''

Beth turned in her bucket seat and stared at the man behind the wheel. ''You can't mean that, Martin. How could his seeing me jeopardize his position at the hospital? Either he's chief resident material or he's not. Either he deserves the cardiovascular fellowship or he doesn't.''

''Don't be so naive,'' Martin said. ''You surely realize how political such appointments can be. Sky has already made an enemy out of Richard Christenson. He still has my support, but to be perfectly honest, if he compromised your effectiveness as a fund-raiser for Healing Arts, I would withdraw it.''

''That's blackmail,'' Beth protested. ''You can't run people's lives like that.''

''I put the welfare of the Healing Arts Medical Center above other considerations, Beth,'' he said as he executed a smooth turn with his Mercedes onto La Jolla Boulevard. ''I am dedicated to seeing that it occupies as significant a place in medicine as Justin envisioned when he first shared his dream with me back in our medical school days.''

''Is it all just to fulfill Justin's dream?'' Beth asked accusingly. ''It seems to me you're on a real power trip, Martin. You want Healing Arts to be important because that makes you important.''

Her words were angering him. The glare of oncoming headlights revealed a throbbing vein in his throat, a tightness in his jaw. The tires spun on the gravel shoulder of the road as he turned into her drive.

"I always put Healing Arts first," he said between clenched teeth. "I've used some of the foundation's discretionary funds and arranged to have your house payments brought current and your property taxes taken care of. In return, I expect you to act like a respectable widow lady. And I don't want to see you in that white number that you're wearing ever again. The kind of widow lady I'm talking about doesn't wear clothes that show her curves."

Beth didn't even bother with a good-night. She exited the car and slammed the door behind her. Her headache was terrible. Even her teeth hurt.

Martin followed her to the door. "Let's not fight, Beth," he said, grabbing her arm. They stood in a pool of yellow from the porch light. The light gave Martin's snow-white hair an unattractive orange cast. "I realize this is tough for you, that you feel some sort of urge to put your past behind you and seek your future. But your responsibility to the past has not ended. You must work with me and the Wisharts and the board members on this fund drive. You are our living link with Justin. You are our most valuable asset right now. If you become involved with another man, you would not only no longer be an asset, you would cause incalculable harm to the whole drive. Successful fund-raising is based on emotional appeal. People get caught up in a swell of nostalgia or gratitude or a crusading spirit or proving their own self-worth—all sorts of reasons, all of them emotional and therefore capricious. An outpouring of goodwill can change to cool indifference overnight just by something as simple as the widow of the saint becoming involved with another man. Don't do this to Healing Arts, Beth—at least not until we get this wing funded.''

Beth took a deep breath of the sea air in a futile attempt to clear her head of the throbbing. "I never said I wouldn't be there for you, Martin. But when will it end? After the Cynthia Wishart Memorial Research Wing and the Justin Dunning Memorial Medical Library, what will come next? Justin used to talk of a children's hospital, of a geriatric facility, of an extended-care facility, of genetic research, of an empire."

Beth let herself in the empty house and stood with her back against the door, waiting for the sound of Martin's departing car. She dropped her purse on the floor and half staggered into the living room.

The remains of the party were everywhere. It was overwhelming. The smell of liquor and salmon pâté and stale tobacco assailed her nostrils and brought a wave of nausea. She remembered how she felt when this room was filled with people and the anticipation of Jonathan that had gladdened her and filled her with such vitality. It was all gone now, replaced by disappointment and a headache that pressed on her eyeballs and throbbed at her temples and made her want to cry out in pain.

She paced the room, holding her head, not knowing how to control the pain. She stopped and picked up a dirty glass and looked helplessly around at all the other dirty glasses. At the overflowing ashtrays. The mess. She should be cleaning up the mess. But she couldn't. She couldn't stand to be in the same room with it. The glass slipped from her fingers and shattered as it struck the edge of the coffee table. She stared helplessly at the shards of glass scattered over the carpet. Tomorrow. She'd have to deal with it all tomorrow.

The kitchen was worse. She got an ice cube from the refrigerator and rubbed it across her forehead. She had never had such a headache. Maybe she was going to have a stroke. Maybe there was something organically wrong with her. But as soon as the thought arose in her mind, she discarded it. She knew the pain in her head was only a manifestation of her frustration and the sense of invisible entrapment that pressed in around her as surely as the stone walls of a prison cell pressed in around a convicted criminal.

Disoriented, she stood in the middle of her kitchen, the one in which she had spent so many hours preparing meals for her family and food for guests and running this household from the small desk in the corner. When it was tidy, it was a pleasant room, with hanging plants and an area rug under the breakfast table, a small television set on the cabinet, even an easy chair and ottoman in the corner. Tricia would sit there and watch her television shows and chatter to Beth while she cooked. Justin would sometimes sit there and tell her about his day. It had been a good life. She did not regret it. But she had a sense of something nebulous and vague but wonderful waiting for her outside the confines of this room, of this house, of the domain Justin had created for himself and those attached to him. Tonight, however, a fear had begun to creep into her veins. She felt imprisoned by the past. What if she would never be able to seek out that vague, wonderful something new.

When the fact that the doorbell was ringing finally registered, she realized that it had rung twice before.

Jonathan had come. Was she surprised? No, she decided. Not really. Just because her anticipation had been replaced by pain and resignation didn't mean that he had given up on the unspoken promises they had exchanged during the first part of the evening.

When she opened the door, he swept across the threshold and engulfed her in his arms. "Ah, Beth, my darling Beth, I want you. I'm not sure what's going to happen with us, but I want you so very much."

His lips sought hers, but in an instant he drew back, sensing something was amiss. He stared at her.

"What the hell...?"

"I can't. My head..." That was all she could say. Such an effort to say just that much.

Then his arms went around her once again, but gently now. Strong arms being ever so gentle. The skin on his cheek felt cool against her forehead.

"Ah, my poor Beth," he whispered over and over. "Don't let them do this to you. Don't."

He carried her down the hall. *Déjà vu,* she thought through the ever-increasing pain, remembering that other time when he had carried her down this hall. Only tonight there would be no passion. The passion had died, or rather, it had been killed. Responsibility, duty, old debts, guilt—like snipers from behind their trees, the four had ambushed her passion and left it dying in a ditch.

With such care, Jonathan lowered her onto the bed.

Soon there was a wet cloth on her forehead. She tried to lie still and soak in its coolness, but the pain made her thrash about. She could not hold back the groans. The pain was ghastly. The word "migraine" crossed her mind. Her mother had migraines. Was this one of those headaches? No wonder her mother had feared them so. No wonder her mother had been so handicapped.

She could hear Jonathan in the bathroom, searching through the medicine cabinet. When he returned to the bed, he helped her to a sitting position and gave her a pill to swallow. She didn't ask what it was.

He sat beside her until the drug calmed her. When she quieted, he removed her clothing, leaving only her undergarments. Then he covered her with a sheet and began to rub her temples and scalp with deft, caring fingers. Beth wasn't sure whether the healing was coming from his fingertips or from the drug dispensing itself throughout her body. But whatever, the pain began to recede. It did not go away, but somehow her ability to bear it had been greatly increased, and she was able to put it at a distance.

Finally, she knew she would sleep. Jonathan knew it, too. He stretched out beside her on the bed and cradled her in his arms. Beth wondered if this was to be the one night in an entire lifetime she would sleep in Jonathan's arms.

Tears instantly sprang to her eyes and poured out onto his shoulder. He wiped them away with his fingers.

Beth wanted to tell him that she loved him, but she wasn't sure she had the right. Their relationship was still so undefined. So she didn't say the words out loud. She only thought them. *I love you, Jonathan Sky.* Over and over the words repeated themselves in her mind until she slept.

The red numbers on the digital clock announced it was two-thirty when she came back from her drug-induced sleep. The headache was an unpleasant, dull ache encasing her head. But it was nothing like before.

Her mouth sought his throat. She could feel his appreciative murmur through her lips.

"How do you feel?" he asked.

"Better, but still terrible. Could I have another pill—maybe just a half this time?"

The water tasted wonderful. She drank the entire glass.

Then Jonathan had her stretch out on her stomach, and he rubbed her back and shoulders and neck for what seemed like an eternity. Beth was floating.

Slowly she turned over and began to unbutton his shirt.

"Are you sure, Beth? You don't have to do this," he said. "I find great joy in just being here with you and caressing you."

"I know you do. I can tell. But I want you to make love to me, Jonathan," she said, pulling the shirt away from his shoulders.

Then she remembered. "I'm not..." She hesitated, not wanting to say the words that would keep him from her. "I'm not using any sort of birth control," she admitted.

"No problem," he said. "I'll take care of it. As you so wisely pointed out, it is possible for men to take some initiative in that department."

On this evening, passion was indeed dead. But it had been replaced by something more caring and profound. And sweet. So incredibly sweet Beth wondered if one could die of it.

He was so unhurried with her, so absolutely insistent that she be the focus of their lovemaking. He wanted only to please her. He dedicated his every touch and word to that end.

How could he know her body better than she knew it herself? How could he know what she would like, what would bring stabs of sweet ecstasy shooting through her body?

He demanded no response from her but pleasure. When she protested that she felt selfish, he said, "It's I who am being selfish. You can't imagine how I enjoy seeing the pleasure in your face, feeling it in your body. Enjoy, my precious Beth. You deserve it. I think I'm just beginning to understand how much you deserve it."

"You know, then, that I've never been able to respond very much sexually. This is all new to me."

"You've never had it completely, have you?" he asked.

"I don't think I can, Jonathan, but just to have these feelings that you are giving me fills me with such wonder."

Yes, such wonder, Beth thought. That his lips on her breasts could bring such exquisite feelings—feelings that radiated downward, filling her with desire. Perhaps the greatest wonder was the abandonment with which her body welcomed his touch, his mouth, his kisses.

She began to long for him to enter her. It was incredible how open she felt, how intensely her emotional yearning transferred itself into a physical need.

"I want you now," she told him. And she did. She really did want this man, this one man in all the world. She wanted to enter with him into the most intimate of human experiences. She wanted him to make love to her.

"No, not yet, darling Beth. Not yet," he told her.

With such gentleness and understanding, he teased her body to an even higher plane of sensation. She was out of herself now, floating out with him in space, abandoning all the old inhibitions, all the old fears and restrictions. She could almost feel the layers from the past falling away from her one by one. With Jonathan, it was as though the past had never been. She was brand-new. A bride for his manhood. And when he finally took her, a feeling of exquisite warmth burst open deep inside her, and like a pebble thrown into a still pond, began to radiate circles of pure sensation. Circle after circle after circle, widening ever outward into infinity. Her whole body, her entire being, was taken with the radiating circles of sexual fulfillment—through her belly, her breasts, her inner thighs, her legs and arms, until it exited finally through her fingers and toes and gave her peace.

It was the greatest peace she had ever known.

FIRST LIGHT WAS PEEKING through the drawn drapes. Jonathan would have to leave her soon.

As though in denial, he moved his body still closer to hers. Her warm, soft body was arousing, but he ignored his desire. She needed to sleep off the headache and the medication.

He felt so tender toward her, so completely in love. God, what in the hell had he done, falling in love with her of all people? Why not the governor's wife? Or the mother superior at a convent? Neither of those women would have been any less appropriate than Beth.

Yet he resented the outside powers that had the right to say whom he was and was not to love—the powers that had decided it suited their purposes for Beth Dunning to be unofficially canonized.

The good Widow Dunning giving her saintly blessing to all who contributed to the "cause." The Mother Teresa of Healing Arts. Martin Morrison and crew had really set her up. She was their number-one public relations ploy. People would never forget how Justin Dunning had rushed across a continent to save her life. They were fascinated by the romance of her story. And Jonathan had watched how people responded to her. There was something so naturally dignified about her demeanor, something so otherworldly about her unassuming beauty that almost went unnoticed at first, and then one looked again and was stunned. People had transferred their awe of Dr. Dunning to the feet of his widow. They needed recognition for their gifts of tribute to Healing Arts. They needed Beth to give her blessing and tell them how good they were.

And if it became known that the saint was having an affair with one of her dead husband's disciples, all hell would break loose for her and him both.

Yet he couldn't stand what they were doing to her. He found himself wishing he could transfer to another residency program. It was too late for that now, however. If he didn't complete his residency here at Healing Arts, he could forget a cardiovascular fellowship. And if he transferred at this late stage of the game, he'd be the last man on the totem pole, not chief resident. He didn't like being under the control of others, especially men he did not admire.

Jonathan realized that he was caught in the middle of a power struggle between the old guard and those who wanted to be the new.

What if it all came down around his ears, Jonathan wondered as he cradled the sleeping woman in the curve of his own body. How would he feel about falling short of his goal after all these years of aiming for the summit?

Beth stirred. Had anything ever felt more right than the curve of her back against his body?

And this woman, he pondered. Where did she fit in? Jonathan didn't know that.

His hand rested on the underside of her breasts where they swelled abruptly and rose into soft mounds. He relished the sensation. He closed his eyes to visualize that special place. So beautiful. So totally feminine and alluring. And Beth didn't even know that he adored that part of her. She didn't know how the sight of her upturned hand on the pillow next to her face filled him with wonder. And her hair, soft against his face. He drank in its scent.

He thought of their lovemaking. He knew that Beth had never experienced the completeness that lovemaking could bring. He had given her that gift. How proud that made him, but how sad that she had lived so much of her life locked in a passionless marriage.

In the early hours of the morning, however, he had fulfilled her. Together they had left all barriers far behind and entered a private paradise. It was the most total experience of his life.

Somehow, being with Beth made him think of home, of smogless skies, of magnificent thunderheads building proudly on the distant horizon, of the prairie with its waving grass and stands of stubborn cottonwoods, of the uncomplicated beauty with which he had grown up.

He wanted her in a way now that transcended mere sexual need. He wanted to merge with her, to become one being with her. His insides contorted with this new desire. In his mind he was with her on a high bluff, at their feet the vast prairie where his people once hunted the buffalo. And they made love there on a soft doeskin laid across the breast of Oklahoma's red earth, her winds caressing them. Like an ancient ritual, their lovemaking was a celebration of all that could be. It was elemental and pure.

Never in his life had Jonathan wanted a woman more than he wanted Beth at that moment.

But her sleep was deep and sound. He loved her enough to leave her alone. There would be another time for them.

Chapter Nine

Beth awakened and remembered.

Instantly, she reached over for Jonathan, but he was gone. She kept her hand on the indentation in the pillow where his head had rested. If only she could have touched him before he left her. It was so lonely without him. How strange. The room had never felt emptier.

She looked at the digital clock on her bedside table. It reported the time as 6:14. So early. But he had probably been gone for some time already. He was to scrub on the first case. That meant he needed to be in surgery by six-thirty.

Beth felt a stab of resentment that he wasn't here.

She sighed and stretched. "Get involved with another surgeon," she said into the empty room, "and you still don't have anyone to drink your morning coffee with." And she needed that—something small and normal to balance the emotional high of last night.

Last night.

Beth groaned. She had been to the other side of the moon and back. Dangerous stuff. She had gone from wanting a man to needing him.

She rolled over and got out of bed. A residual twinge of pain reminded her of her headache. Her mouth was cottony from the medication. When she stood, her legs were wobbly. She put on a robe and headed for the kitchen to get her coffee.

The phone rang as she poured her second cup. She dared hope it was Jonathan. But no. He would be in surgery.

It was a nurse.

"Dr. Sky asked me to call," the nurse explained, her tone curious. "He wanted to make sure you were over your headache."

"I'm fine," Beth said. "Thank you."

Jonathan himself called just before eleven. He sounded rushed. "I've only got a minute. I'm on second call tonight and can't leave the grounds. But I wondered if you would be willing to share bread and wine and candlelight with me in my shabby quarters."

She forgave him for being gone when she woke up. Her heart soared. "That sounds wonderful."

"I can't get away to shop. Would you mind bringing the bread and the wine? And the candle?" he added sheepishly.

"No problem. I'll bring some fruit, too."

"Beth," he said, his voice hesitant, "maybe I shouldn't even ask you to come. I might have to leave. But I want to see you so much, it's like I have a disease."

"I know," she said. "I'll risk it."

"Risk what? My not being there or catching my disease?"

"Both."

He was there—for exactly five minutes. They didn't even get the candle lit before the phone call came from the emergency room, taking him away from her. Before she left Jonathan's apartment, she called Tricia to see if her daughter was interested in going to a movie. But Kimmie was with Tricia, and they were making fudge. Then they were going back over to Kimmie's to meet two other girls.

So Beth went to a movie by herself. It was a remake of an old Cary Grant—Ingrid Bergman film. Beth had seen the original on television. It was far superior to the new version.

I need a job and some friends, she thought on the way home. The people she had previously thought of as her friends she now realized were really Justin's colleagues and their wives. A single woman did not fit into that world. Other than activities related to Healing Arts, Beth had no social life.

Yes, she definitely had to do something about her life. And allowing it to once again revolve around a physician did not seem a good solution.

Or would it be possible to structure a life that had both a physician husband and a life of her own?

When Jonathan came to the house for hamburgers on Tuesday evening, Beth insisted that Tricia be there. Tricia was sullen. Beth tried a variety of topics, attempting to draw Tricia into a conversation with Jonathan and make her feel wanted. When Jonathan asked her questions about her school and her friends, she answered in as few words as possible. Jonathan acted almost relieved when the inevitable phone call came from the hospital. He volunteered to stop by and look at a patient that evening when the person on the other end had obviously said in the morning would be soon enough.

The following Friday was the beginning of Jonathan's two-week vacation. It afforded him and Beth the opportunity to spend long hours together with the Dunning papers. Their project legitimized their being together, postponing any need to make decisions about their relationship.

Beth wasn't ready to decide what came next. She wanted only to live each day as it came, to enjoy the knowledge that when she woke up in the morning that she would be with Jonathan during that day. She'd worry about what came next at the end of the two weeks, or at the end of the book project. Any decision could be put off until then. It was as though they had an unspoken agreement. No matter what came afterward, they would have had these two weeks.

After only two days, they had established small, comforting rituals. She knew when he cleared his throat, that he was about to read her something. He would reach out and touch her whenever she walked by his chair—so small a gesture, but it meant so much. At ten-thirty, they would break for coffee on the terrace. At lunch, he made the tea while she fixed sandwiches. In the evening, they fixed simple meals together. After dinner they would take a walk on the beach, then return to work for a while longer. They ended the day with a swim. It was with reluctance that she bid Jonathan goodbye at night. It seemed unnatural to be sending him home. He belonged in bed with her. But there was Tricia to consider.

Beth's chief concern over her daughter, however, was not the lack of privacy her presence in the house brought, but Tricia's behavior. Her daughter's reaction to having Jonathan in the house every day made Beth very uncomfortable.

Tricia would disappear to her room whenever Jonathan appeared, and she did not come out until he left unless it was to leave the house herself. She refused their invitations to take meals with them, always saying she wasn't hungry.

When they invited her on an evening drive down to Tijuana, she said she needed to wash her hair. When Jonathan asked her to come with them on a Sunday evening drive up to Palomar Observatory, she curtly informed him that she had other plans.

"I wish you'd make more of an effort to be polite to Dr. Sky," Beth finally said at breakfast after almost a week of this behavior.

"What'd I do?" Tricia whined. "Can't I go to my own room when I want?"

"Not when it's intended as an obvious affront to a guest in this house," Beth said firmly.

"He's your friend, not mine."

"I don't disappear in my room when your friends come around."

"That's different," Tricia said defiantly.

"Why is it different?"

"It just is," Tricia said, shoving back her plate and chair with one motion. "I'm going down to the beach."

Beth watched out the window as Tricia walked straightbacked across the terrace toward the steps that led down the cliff to the beach below. She was at a loss to know how to handle the petulant teenager. Tricia made her angry, but Beth was wise enough to understand that her daughter's behavior was a result of her feelings of insecurity. The teenager did not understand just where Dr. Sky fit into their lives. And Beth wasn't sure herself.

Beth cleaned up the kitchen first and then went to shower and dress before Jonathan arrived. They tried to get an early start each day, determined to make the most of Jonathan's vacation time.

They worked diligently on the tedious editing project. How difficult it was to select from the voluminous journals and letters just the right passages to illustrate the life of Justin Dunning and the emergence of the Healing Arts Foundation and Medical Center. Without actually talking about it, they both seemed to understand they were not expected to put together a true portrait of the man—that this book was to glorify the legend and serve as a public relations tool for the medical center.

Finally, however, Jonathan couldn't resist saying, "He gave up so much in pursuit of greatness. He was in many ways less complete as a human being because of it. I never before considered what a trade-off it is. It makes me wonder if greatness is worth it. These journals of your husband's show a man who to my way of thinking had either lost the human touch or was afraid of being human. The journals are so incomplete. So one-sided."

"Yes," Beth agreed. "He created this incredible public persona for himself that allowed for no signs of weakness, no indecision, no agonizing. Maybe that's what robbed him of his humanity. What a burden it must have been always to appear to be perfect. I wish I'd understood this earlier. Maybe I could have helped him be more human."

Jonathan reached over and touched her hand. "No looking back, Beth. We can't revise history."

"But it colors our present and our future. How can we help but regret past mistakes?"

"I think we should learn from the past and use it to create the future," he told her. "But in a way I guess the only true mistake is not to learn from the past. Nobody starts out to err. We all do what we think we need to do, or what we thought best at the time."

"I'll never regret this time spent with you," Beth told him, drinking in every detail of his exotic features. "No matter what comes after, I want to look back on this time as something good."

"I'd like to kiss you now, Beth," Jonathan said softly, his eyes full of longing. "But I'm not going to, because it will just make me want you more."

Beth smiled and touched his cheek. She understood. Tricia was in the house; they were not alone. But how it pleased her to know that he wanted her. And how she wanted him. So little time they could spend alone together, but she thought of him every single minute they were apart. She was crazily in love with the Indian surgeon from Oklahoma, and she didn't know what to do about it or where it would lead. She wasn't sure if she should make any more changes in Tricia's life at this point. She felt a responsibility toward Healing Arts, and the role she seemed destined to play with the fund-raising project dictated that she do nothing to tarnish her image as the grieving widow forever dedicated to her husband's mission. She understood that Jonathan's getting involved with her, or with any other woman complicated his very tightly scheduled and financially restricted life. And she suspected that if Jonathan's and her special relationship became public knowledge, it would jeopardize his appointment as chief resident. Many people would be scandalized if they found out she was having an affair with one of her husband's residents. She hated the deceit, but she was trapped by it.

Perhaps the unique set of problems that stood in their way was a blessing of sorts. It kept them from rushing into something they might regret later. They were in the throes of beginning a new, exciting relationship. But that did not mean they should make a life together.

She stared at the photographs on the wall of the study documenting Justin's dramatic and colorful life. She was in some of them—in the background or off to one side. Some of the photographs she had been cropped out of altogether. In others, just her hand or coattail was barely visible at the edge of the picture, reminding Beth that she had been there when it was taken. Did she want that again—to be a background wife? She did not regret her marriage to Justin, but if she married again, she would want a more clear-cut identity of her own. And to do that she would probably have to marry a different kind of man.

Beth understood that she and Jonathan were both living in the present, looking forward only to the next time they were together. Neither of them was ready to deal with the future. But how glorious it was when they were together.

He touched her hand, reclaiming her from her thoughts. She looked down at his hand over hers. How beautiful. A layer of mist formed over her eyes, because the sight of his hand touching her was so beautiful.

At dusk, they took their walk on the beach. Safely out of sight of the house, they linked arms and shared the sunset in silence.

Somehow the awesome, relentless sea was less intimidating to Beth with this man at her side. She felt safe and happy and could appreciate its beauty. The waves were gentle and rhythmic as they rolled over the glistening sand. The sky filled itself with a palette of colors ranging from the softest of pinks to the most blatant of corals. The gulls were silhouetted against the sky as they swooped downward to dive for their dinner and called to one another while floating effortlessly on the currents of air. The breezes teased her hair and brought the perfume of the sea to her nostrils.

It was so beautiful, this moment with the wonders of nature and this compelling man, and her heart filled with such love for him—just a tiny moment in eternity that would quickly pass but was so achingly lovely it brought her pain. *So full of ironies, this life we lead,* Beth thought. *We can build a wall around ourselves and live safely. Then there is no pain, but there's no beauty, either. One is the price for the other.* And if the price she had to pay for finding this moment was someday to suffer the pain of losing Jonathan Sky, then it would have been worth it.

If there was no way to make a life with this man, she would never regret having loved him. Never. He had given her back herself.

They walked out on a decaying wooden pier and sat at its end. And they talked.

"If you were queen of the world," he asked, "what changes would you make?"

He was like that—always asking her questions that made her think. Beth never ceased to marvel at the wonderful conversations they had. Not only did they long to share their bodies with one another, but they had a mutual desire to share their minds. He was so well-read and so wise. It was incredible to her that he wanted to know her opinion on everything. He cared about what she thought! He forced her to formulate opinions on things she had never bothered to evaluate before—political and religious issues, art, music, books. He played the devil's advocate and forced her to defend her position. At times, she found herself actually in heated arguments with him. It was amazing. She had always avoided arguments before, always deferred to the male opinion.

Jonathan Sky. Was he real? Could any man be this wonderful?

He had the body of a warrior, the hands of a surgeon and the heart of a poet. She knew she could never love another man more.

He saw the love in her eyes and took her in his arms. He kissed her lips lightly, then drew back as though to reaffirm the look in her eyes. He kissed her again. And again. Each time the urgency of his passion became more evident. Beth pressed her body against him, responding. Her kisses matched his—eager, penetrating kisses that asked for more and more. Consuming kisses that held nothing back, that blended lips and tongue and longing into an act so incredibly personal and intimate that it left them both weak.

"Now. I want you now," Beth whispered, although whispers were unnecessary. They shared this place only with the restless gulls and the strange little crustaceans that scurried along the beach.

And there, in a secluded place, screened by the marsh grasses, cradled by sand still warm from its day in the sunshine, they made love. It seemed altogether fitting and proper that they unite themselves in this place of untouched nature, their cries of passion mingling with the music of the sea. As elemental as the ocean, as primitive as the creatures that inhabited it, as pure as the sand on its beaches, as ferocious as its winds, their love filled them, flowing and ebbing like the tides, coming in wave upon wave until they floated into calm waters and found quiet contentment in each other's arms.

"I didn't know it could be like this," Beth said, wondering if she had just trespassed into some paradise where mere mortals were not supposed to go. What if after discovering this glory, it was taken away from her? She had an incredible sense of foreboding about this love she shared with Jonathan Sky. It was too rare and wild and wonderful. Something like that could not last. It was like the brilliant sunset they had just witnessed—a moment of beauty that would inevitably pass.

BETH TOOK HER SKIRT from the chair by Jonathan's desk. She paused to look over the impressive array of medical textbooks stacked on the cluttered desk and on the shelf above it. She looked around the tiny, Spartan efficiency apartment that was Jonathan's home. In a building adjacent to the hospital, the apartment was one of those furnished to the resident staff.

Over the sofa was a breathtaking oil painting of an eagle in flight. The splendid painting looked too grand for its functional surroundings. Beth knew without asking that it was by Jonathan's father. The bold signature in the corner proudly proclaimed it as the work of Billy Joe Sky. "He was young when he painted it and still believed in the future," Jonathan explained.

"Then he started cranking out hack stuff for the tourists."

An Indian rug covered the floor, the only other unique touch to the drab apartment.

But while they had made love on the bed in its tiny alcove, this place had been the most special in the universe.

"I'm sorry I can't court you properly," Jonathan told her as he watched her dress. "I should be taking you to elegant places. You should be made love to on satin sheets instead of hospital cotton. You should be wined and dined in expensive restaurants and not fed carry-out fare from the local delicatessen. You should—"

Beth walked over to where he sat on the edge of the bed and hushed him with a finger to his lips. "I've had elegant. It didn't make me happy," she told him. "*You* make me happy."

But even as she said the words, a great sadness overtook Beth. True, she was happy on the occasions when they could come here and be alone. But their meetings were always clandestine. Intimacy was impossible at her house because of Tricia. Beth wasn't ready to flaunt her relationship with Jonathan in front of her confused and insecure stepdaughter. Neither she nor Jonathan could afford hotels. And here, on the grounds of Healing Arts, they had to be careful that no one saw them together.

Beth resented the entire situation. It seemed so ridiculous for two unmarried adults to be put in the position of sneaking around to be together. But if certain people found out one of the residents was having an affair with her, it would stir up a hornet's nest for both

of them. And as Martin Morrison pointed out, it
could damage the fund drive for the new wing.

Beth was weary of the fund drive. In the weeks that
followed Jonathan's vacation, she had been paraded
around to civic clubs, county medical meetings,
women's clubs and service organizations in order to
make appeals for their support of the Cynthia Wishart Memorial Research Wing. She and Martin had also
flown to a half-dozen other cities to make their pitch
before the nation's various philanthropic foundations. Beth felt like a wind-up doll, programmed to
act, speak and dress according to the dictates of Martin Morrison, the Wisharts and the various board
members involved in the fund-raising project.

In a way, Justin had created a monster out of the
Healing Arts Foundation. The bigger and more important it became, the more money that was needed to
feed its insatiable appetite. While Beth did not doubt
the worthy research and healing that was being accomplished by Healing Arts, it sometimes seemed to
her that its primary mission was raising money. Already on the drawing board were plans for even more
expansion, and the money was not yet raised for the
present project. The creation of a world-class medical
center was a worthy cause, but the egos of Martin and
the others were so intimately involved with Healing
Arts that Beth often felt they lost sight of the real
purpose. It had become a project to make them more
powerful and important. Or in the case of the Wisharts, Healing Arts was also part of an attempt to im-
mortalize their beloved daughter. Beth wondered what
they would do when the research wing was completed
and they were forced at last to face the void she left in
their lives.

The words over the gate at the entrance to the Healing Arts grounds said, "That more may live longer and healthier lives through the advancement of medicine." It did not say, "That a few may grow influential through the creation of a monument to themselves, or to the memory of their dead child."

And Beth had come to regard Healing Arts as a monster in another sense. In addition to its insatiable appetite for money, Healing Arts dominated her life. Betty Wishart had said that Beth was the living embodiment of Justin Dunning. And how they had traded on that.

Her involvement with Healing Arts robbed Beth of her personality, her identity. But when she was with this very special man who sat on the bed where they had just made love and with loving eyes watched her dress, through him, she was beginning to have a sense of who and what she was.

Jonathan, however, was following in Justin's footsteps. If she made a life with him, would she lose her newly found self all over again? Was it wrong to want some accolades of her own? But after so long a time of doing for someone else, she actually had very little notion of what she would do with her life on her own.

"Where's my blouse?" she said, looking around the tiny apartment. "I could have sworn I wore one in here."

Jonathan picked it up from a tangle of covers at the foot of the bed. He held it in both his hands and buried his face in it, inhaling her scent from the cloth.

Beth watched in disbelief. She still could not believe that a man was so captivated by her that he would do such a thing. He looked up at her as he handed her the crumpled garment. But when she reached for it, he dropped it on the bed and grabbed her hand. He kissed the back of her hand, then turned it over and kissed her wrist.

Her wrist had never been kissed before.

He kissed the tip of each finger. He buried his mouth in her palm.

With her free hand she touched his shining black hair. No matter what happened, she would remember these times with Jonathan for the rest of her life. He was a part of her now.

The phone rang on Jonathan's bedside table. Beth listened while he spoke efficiently to the nurse on the other end of the line. An emergency in the making. Jonathan hung up the phone and was instantly on his feet, jerking on his clothes. He was no longer her lover; the physician in him had taken over. At least this time the phone hadn't rung in the middle of their lovemaking. In the time it took Beth to put on her stockings, he had finished dressing, given her a peck on the cheek and was at the door.

"Will you be at the reception tomorrow night?" Beth called after him.

"Morrison has decreed it a command performance. Maybe we can sneak off somewhere and neck," he called back and then was gone.

Beth smiled at the thought of sneaking off to neck at the Wishart mansion. The affair tomorrow night would be elegant, spared from being black tie only because Martin reminded Betty Wishart that many on the Healing Arts staff probably did not own formal clothes.

Beth finished dressing and slipped out into the hall, nervously checking up and down its length to see if anyone would catch her leaving Dr. Sky's apartment.

No, she didn't like sneaking around one bit. Something was going to have to change.

TRICIA WAS NOT AT HOME.

Beth thought nothing of her daughter's absence until dinnertime arrived.

When she looked in Tricia's room, it took her only a minute to decide what was wrong.

Justin's picture was missing from the bedside table. The small album that held pictures of Tricia's mother was gone from the top of her bureau.

Beth looked in the closet. Tricia's suitcase was gone. And some of her clothes.

"Oh, my God," Beth said as the implication sank in.

She raced to the telephone.

Kimmie hadn't seen Tricia all day. No, she didn't know where Tricia was. Her voice sounded surprised. "Is anything wrong?"

"I'll call you later and explain," Beth said.

Tricia was not at her grandmother's.

Should she call the police or go out and look for her? Beth's hands were shaking as she rubbed her forehead. What to do? She felt panic gnawing at her chest and throat. What to do?

She reached for the phone again. She misdialed and tried again.

"I'm sorry," the nurse said. "Dr. Sky is scrubbed in on a case. It will be several hours until he can come to the phone. May I take a message?"

Beth wanted to scream. She wanted Jonathan. Now. Tricia had run away. She didn't want to face this by herself.

"Ma'am, do you want to leave a message?" the nurse repeated.

Beth knew if she left a message for Dr. Sky to call her, the news would be all over the hospital. Nothing spread faster than gossip through a hospital.

"Yes. Tell him to call Beth Dunning. As soon as possible. It's an emergency.

By the time Jonathan called, the police had come and gone. Another teenage runaway did not impress them very much. Obviously, no crime had been committed. Tricia's grandmother and the Wisharts were seated with Beth in the living room. Martin Morrison was in the kitchen, fixing sandwiches that no one would eat. A neighbor had brought over a cake. Beth wanted to tell the woman to take it back home. Neighbors bringing in food made her think of funerals.

Betty Wishart was sniffling. "I know how you feel, Beth. I know what it's like to lose your little girl." She grabbed Beth's hand and started patting it.

Beth pulled her hand away. She was about to insist the Wisharts leave when the phone rang with Jonathan's call.

Beth explained. Her voice broke at the words "run away."

"I'll be right over—just as soon as I get someone to take care of my patient," Jonathan said.

"Right over," however, was more than an hour later.

There was still no word about Tricia when he arrived. The others had left.

Beth did not throw herself into Jonathan's arms. She felt distant. She had discovered her daughter was missing almost four hours ago.

"I'm sorry, Beth," Jonathan said when she turned away from his embrace. "But surely you realize that physicians have special demands."

"Yes, I know. God, how I know," Beth said, biting her lip to keep from crying. Where in the hell had Tricia gone? She should be doing something to find her.

"Hey, Beth," Jonathan said, taking her hand. "It's me, Jonathan. I'd slay dragons for you. I'd face a raging tiger. Anything else. But I can't run out on a critical patient until I arrange coverage."

Beth looked at his face. He was right, of course. But although part of her wanted to tell him to go away, that she had managed for the past four hours without him, another part of her was glad that he had come at last.

"Oh, Jonathan, where is she?" Beth asked. And she allowed him to hold her, smooth her hair, to kiss her brow.

He sat with her throughout the night. Beth hated the inaction. She felt as if she should be out searching, doing anything except sitting here on the sofa. But she felt that she needed to be by the phone in case Tricia called, or the police. She hated to think of what a call from the police might mean.

In the quiet house, Jonathan listened to Beth's fears, her list of all the terrible things that could happen to young girls. He didn't treat her like a child, telling her not to worry, that everything would be all right. Instead, he said, "She's a bright kid, Beth. Chances are she has enough sense to keep herself out of trouble. But you have every right to be worried."

And he told her that he would stay with her as long as he could, that he would be at her side no matter what happened.

But Beth knew that was not necessarily so. At some point, Jonathan would have to return to the hospital. If something dreadful happened, she might very well have to face it alone.

Chapter Ten

It was dawn when the door bell rang. Beth jumped as if she'd been shot. As she ran across the entry hall to the front door, she knew it was either good news or bad. No one would ring the door bell at this hour to report on nothing.

She paused a second to collect herself, then threw open the door.

Tricia was standing beside an oversized uniformed policeman. A patrol car was parked behind them in the driveway.

Wordlessly, Beth opened her arms. Tricia let out a gasp as if she had been holding her breath for a very long time and fell against her stepmother. She buried her face against Beth's shoulder and sobbed. "I'm sorry. It was a dumb thing to do."

"Found her at the bus station," the policeman said. "She was just sittin' there. Didn't have a ticket or anything."

"I didn't have any money for a ticket," Tricia said, lifting her tear-streaked face and looking at Beth beseechingly. "And no place to go. I don't know why I did such a stupid thing. I mean, I was afraid of—of things," she said, her voice suddenly guarded as she caught sight of Jonathan standing off to one side of the spacious entryway.

"What's he doing here?" Tricia demanded, her voice angry.

"I asked him to come," Beth said. "He's been here with me all night—the longest night I've ever spent. I was worried sick, and I needed a friend here with me. Jonathan is my friend, Tricia. And he's yours, too, if you'll let him."

Tricia grabbed her suitcase from the policeman. "Thank you for bringing me home," she said.

Then she turned to her mother. "I haven't slept any. I'm going to bed."

To Jonathan, Tricia said nothing.

The three adults watched Tricia walk resolutely down the hallway.

Beth was weak with relief. Her problems with her daughter were far from over, but at least Tricia was safe.

She thanked the policeman and offered him a cup of coffee, which he refused.

After she closed the door behind the policeman, she stood against it, sagging. Jonathan pulled her to him and wrapped his arms around her. Ah, the feel of him, Beth thought. The good, solid, safe feel of him. She wanted to stay in the protected circle of his arms forever.

But soon he was guiding her down the hall, past Tricia's closed door, to her own bedroom. "To bed with you," he said sternly. "You've got to be exhausted."

"You, too," Beth said, realizing how weary she really was.

"I'm used to long hours," he said.

Soon Beth was stretched out on her bed. Jonathan covered her with a quilt and kissed her forehead. "I'll call you later," he said.

Beth wanted to reach out her arms to him, to cling to him a bit longer, but she could sense his need to get back to his duties at the hospital. He had been away too long. He felt the pull of responsibility. *Damn,* she thought selfishly. But he had been with her all through the grim night.

As soon as Jonathan had left, Beth slipped out of bed and padded down to Tricia's room. Maybe she should be more understanding of Jonathan, she thought. Mothers, above all, should understand about responsibility. Beth knew she could not sleep herself until she knew her troubled daughter was all right.

Softly, she pushed open the door of Tricia's room and tiptoed over to the bed. Tricia was asleep. Justin's picture was back in its accustomed place on the bedside table.

BETH SPENT THE NEXT DAY typing a chapter of what she and Jonathan now referred to as "the manuscript." Tricia was being domestic, vacuuming, baking cookies, cleaning out the hall closet. Beth understood that the troubled teenager was seeking comfort in the normalcy of small things, of being a part of the household.

Twice this morning, Tricia had brought Beth cups of coffee. And they had just eaten a tuna soufflé that she had prepared.

"You want to talk about it yet?" Beth asked.

Tricia shook her head no. "Later."

"You okay?" Beth asked.

Tricia had nodded. "I'm getting there, I think. But don't worry. I won't do anything stupid again. Really I won't."

Beth was back at the typewriter, tired of the job at hand but propelled along by the fact that the end of the project now seemed possible.

She wondered if Justin would approve of what they were doing with his life story. They had selected ten patients from various stages of Justin's career and documented in great detail how Justin had diagnosed and treated their problem. The background of Justin's childhood, training and personal life was woven into the transitional material between these ten segments. It did make dramatic reading and would leave the reader with no doubt about the modern-day miracles accomplished by cardiovascular surgery.

Beth wondered if someone would be writing a book someday about Jonathan Sky. Not only was he entering this most daring field of medicine; he was the first of his people ever to do so. And from what he had shared with her about his background, Beth realized that was a remarkable accomplishment—much more so than if he had been born a white middle-class kid in Omaha or Fort Worth.

And what about herself, Beth wondered. Would she be famous because she had been married to two legends in the course of her lifetime? Somehow the thought didn't please her. She found herself wishing that Jonathan were a bus driver or an attorney. Or if he had to be a doctor, why not a dermatologist? Skin doctors did not have to live from one emergency to the next. They led normal lives. Nine fo five. Dinner at six. Time for the kids. But she never would have met Jonathan if he'd been anything other than who he

was. Their paths had crossed because he was a cardiovascular surgeon in training and she was the widow
of his mentor. Ah, the ironies of life.

Beth had to work hard to concentrate. Her thoughts
kept straying to Tricia and to Jonathan. She dared to
feel hopeful about the girl. And because she knew she
was going to see Jonathan that evening, Beth was distracted by a sense of anticipation. Even though they
would be with a crowd of other people and have no
time to themselves, she would be in the same room
with him. She could look on his exquisitely chiseled
face, hear his voice, feel his presence. Being with him
under any circumstances was better than not being
with him at all.

When it came time to get dressed, Beth agonized
over what to wear to the Wisharts' reception honoring the hospital staff who had donated their time to
work on the telethon. Such decisions used to be so
easy. And it seemed trivial to have to worry about such
mundane issues after the trauma of Tricia's brief dis-
appearance. But she had to wear something, and trivial or not, she wanted to look nice.

Beth's clothes were all pretty much the same—conservative, uniformlike. A well-made blazer or suit for
daytime, a navy crepe or its equivalent for evening.
Now she didn't want to be conservative. She didn't
want to wear the uniform of the well-to-do matron.
Such clothing no longer appealed to her. She didn't
want to look like everyone else. She wanted to look
like herself, whoever that was. But she had no money
for new clothes. One of the old standbys would have
to do.

She eyed the navy crepe. Maybe without the de-
mure little lace collar? No, it would still look like

something one wore to church. She pulled out a rose-colored suit. It looked like the mother of the bride. Of course, there were always the white evening pajamas that Martin said clung too much. But they looked like a hostess outfit, and she wasn't the hostess tonight.

Beth wandered to the hall closet, where outdated or out-of-season clothes were banished, to see if there was some forgotten garment that might help her out. There was a rather smart black suit whose skirt had once been deemed too short. But fashion permitted shorter skirts this season. And instead of a proper little white blouse with a bow, maybe the top of the white pajamas might look a little more interesting. With black patent heels and lots of pearls.

The diagonal drape of the silky pullover top looked dramatic with the suit. The pearls were smashing. She pushed up the sleeves of the suit and added gold bracelets. And earrings. Why, she actually looked chic, Beth realized.

She looked down at the skirt length to reassure herself that it wasn't too short and noticed the slit on the side seam. When she bought the skirt, she had stitched closed the ten-inch slit until it was a modest four or five inches. Beth laughed out loud. Yes, she had actually sewn the slit in the skirt lest she show a little more leg than would be seemly. She removed the skirt and took great joy in removing those carefully placed stitches. And when she put the skirt back on, she loved the effect. Amazing how much difference that slit made. The whole outfit looked dressier and more dramatic, and yes, sexier. She walked back and forth in front of the mirror, enjoying the sight of her own leg as revealed by the wonderful slit in this wonderful skirt.

Except that now maybe her makeup and hair didn't match the rest of her. She rushed to the bathroom for more eye shadow. She accentuated her cheekbones with blush.

Now for the hair. She leaned over and shook her head. She'd seen Tricia do it a hundred times for that tousled, fuller effect, but she had never tried it herself. She stood up and looked at herself in the mirror. Fantastic. Beth repeated the procedure, with a brush, this time spraying her hair in its upside-down position, then stood upright and shook her head.

"Wow!" she said out loud to her mirror. "Is that really me? Where in the world have you been keeping yourself, lady?"

She went down the hall to the kitchen. Tricia was sprawled in the easy chair, watching television. Beth stood framed in the doorway for effect.

When Tricia looked up, her face broke into a grin. "Gee whiz, Mom. You look incredible."

Then Beth watched her stepdaughter's face cloud. "You're all dolled up for *him*, aren't you?" Tricia said accusingly.

Beth started to deny the truth of Tricia's words. She looked at her watch. She should be on her way, but this was more important, Beth decided, as she sat down on the ottoman and took one of her daughter's hands in both of hers.

"Yes and no, Tricia. I suppose I'm dressed like this partly for the benefit of Jonathan, but mostly I've done it for my own benefit. I honestly think I've never looked better in my life, and that makes me feel good about myself. And I'm just starting to discover that it's okay to feel good about yourself, that it's okay to live for yourself once in a while. But honey, that doesn't change the way I feel about you. I don't know if I have any sort of future with Jonathan Sky. Right now I'm confused about that. I had a good life with your father, but I'm not sure I want to be the wife of another heart surgeon. The one and only thing I'm absolutely sure of is that you and I will always have each other. Always. Okay?"

Tricia looked at Beth, her eyes rimming with tears. "Promise?"

"Cross my heart and hope to die," Beth said solemnly, making an X over her heart in keeping with the ritual from Tricia's childhood. "Your home is with me for as long as you want and need it. And believe me, I wouldn't miss being the grandmother to your babies for anything in the world."

Tricia looked at her with an unsure frown. She wanted to believe.

"I can understand how it makes you uncomfortable for me to be dating," Beth continued. "I'm the mother in your life. I was your father's wife. But Tricia, I'm also a woman who quite frankly is enjoying having a very wonderful man court her. That doesn't make me less your mother, and it doesn't change the fact that I was married to your father for all those years. But as they say, life goes on."

Tricia chewed on her lip for a long minute, then quite suddenly threw herself into Beth's arms with such force she almost knocked her from the footstool. "But *he* won't want me," she sobbed. "I won't have a home. I won't have any family left if Jonathan Sky takes you away from me."

Beth smoothed Tricia's blond, clean-smelling hair and pressed her lips against the girl's forehead. Then,

The two pairs of French doors were open, and many people had spilled out into the lavishly landscaped backyard with its enormous pool. On the other side of the foyer, in the dining room, was a table laden with a dazzling array of delicacies and attended by a uniformed maid. Other maids circulated with carefully arranged trays of hors d'oeuvres. White-coated waiters circulated among the guests, offering glasses of champagne from silver trays. At the grand piano, a tuxedo-clad pianist provided genteel background music for the dozens of conversations taking place throughout the first floor. The party was designed to impress, and judging from the reaction of those around Beth, it was having the desired effect. Other than the practicing physicians and foundation board members, most of those people had never been inside such a house that said "old money" at every turn and had never attended such a lavish party.

Betty Wishart was the picture of the gracious hostess as she introduced Tricia around and accepted praise for her showplace home and lovely party. Tricia looked so eager and fresh in her white linen shift trimmed in heavy ivory lace. Beth had bought the dress for her last year for a school party, which had also been Tricia's first real date. That had been the month before Justin died. When he had seen her in the dress, he had remarked that his little girl looked so grown up. There was surprise in his voice, and Beth thought there was sadness in his eyes. She wondered if he was sad because he realized that Tricia's childhood had passed him by. Justin had missed his own daughter's childhood. Meanwhile, he had been away saving lives and promoting health. Which was more important? One's own child or the needful sick? Beth was glad she wasn't a physician and forced to face that difficult question.

Some people in attendance knew Tricia from having seen her at various hospital functions that she had attended with Beth and her father. But most people she was meeting for the first time.

What a lovely young person my daughter is, Beth thought. Tricia was now perched on the brink of womanhood. In just the past two days, Tricia seemed older. The running-away episode had been a frightening but maturing experience for her.

Beth watched with pride as Tricia's soft smile and sparkling eyes gave delight to all whom she met. With a poignancy that brought a misting of tears to her eyes, Beth wished Justin could be here to watch his daughter. He would be very proud if he could see her now.

But then if Justin were here, Beth realized, Jonathan Sky would not be regarding her with those wondrous eyes from across the room. Sometimes life made no sense at all, for Beth was sincerely sorry Justin was dead but glad to have Jonathan all at the same time.

Betty Wishart, with her arm firmly tucked around Tricia's waist, made her way through the room to where Beth was standing. After a pointed look at the slit in the side of Beth's skirt, she asked, "Is that a new hairdo? Don't you think it's a little young, my dear?"

"No, actually, I don't. The way I wore it before was too old for me."

"I see," the woman said, unconsciously smoothing her own carefully coiffed hair with her free hand. Then, seeming to remember who was imprisoned in the curve of her right arm, and giving a squeeze to Tricia's waist, she said, "Do you realize Tricia is only a few years older than my Cynthia would have been? What a joy it must be to have such a lovely daughter." The expression on the woman's face changed to a wistful one, and she sighed.

"Yes, Tricia is a joy," Beth agreed. "She is not only my daughter but my dearest friend."

Mrs. Wishart looked distant, then plucked a handkerchief from her pocket and dabbed at her eyes with her free hand. "I just don't understand why my baby had to die, why I couldn't have had her here beside me." She sighed, then began sobbing softly. "You just can't imagine how difficult it has been for me without her."

Tricia looked very uncomfortable from her position next to the crying woman.

Beth stepped forward and took Tricia's hand.

"I see someone I want to introduce my daughter to, but first is there any way we can help you?"

"No, no. Just mingle," Mrs. Wishart said with a brave little smile, and waved them away.

"The poor woman. I feel sorry for her. I know how she must feel," Tricia whispered, looking back at the woman, who had allowed a concerned-looking guest to help her into a chair. Beth knew Tricia was thinking of the pain of losing her father, of facing the fact that she would never see him again.

"How long has her daughter been dead?" Tricia wanted to know.

"Three or four years," Beth answered. "Of course you feel sorry for her, but I don't see you weeping in public because you lost your father. After a point, public displays of grief seem inappropriate," Beth said as they wandered out onto the terrace. "But I think Betty Wishart's making a career out of being the grieving mother, and she certainly seems to have found her calling. I guess that's a trap some people fall into.''

"That's what you don't want to do, isn't it?" Tricia asked. "Make a career out of being Daddy's widow?"

"No, I don't. I don't want to be pitiful like Betty Wishart. I don't want to sound cruel, Tricia, and I am sure she loved her daughter very much. But she doesn't have to prove it to people by weeping in public. She's compounding the child's death by putting her own life and that of her husband on hold, by dedicating her life to the past rather than the future. And by encouraging such behavior in others, she supports her own behavior. In some cultures, they expect bereaved women to wear black for the rest of their lives. Some cultures even expect widows to throw themselves on funeral pyres. People like Mrs. Wishart simply expect widows to stop going forward, to stay in a time warp.

"I wanted you to do that, too—to stay in a time warp," Tricia admitted. "I thought it meant you didn't care about Daddy anymore if you fell in love with another man. I know it sounds dumb but it seemed like Daddy would be more dead somehow if you married someone else—that one of the links to him would be gone."

"I understand your feeling that way," Beth told her daughter as they paused to enjoy the fresh ocean breeze, away from the smoke-filled room. The view was beautiful, with the moonlight on the ocean and the lights from Point Loma twinkling in the distance. "I had to deal with those feelings myself. It felt as if I were making Justin die all over again when I realized that I could go on and have a normal, happy life without him. Tell me; if Mrs. Wishart were to have another child, do you think she would love it?''

"Yes, I guess so," Tricia said, her tone suspicious as she sensed her mother's line of argument.

"Would her loving another child mean she had forgotten about Cynthia?"

"I suppose not," Tricia said reluctantly.

"By dedicating her life to grief, does it make Cynthia any less dead?"

Tricia shrugged her shoulders.

"Tricia, I am not married to your father anymore. I ceased being his wife the instant he died. You can't be married to a dead man. Marriage is a contract between two living people."

"Then you're going to marry Dr. Sky?" Tricia asked, her voice miserable.

"I don't know, honey. The way I feel right now—I love him, and yes, I'd like to be with him for the rest of my life. But things aren't always that simple. Just loving someone doesn't automatically make a marriage appropriate."

"Well, if I got married and really loved the person I was married to and he died, I don't think I could ever marry someone else," Tricia said with a defiant tilt to her chin.

"I think we'd better continue this conversation at another time," Beth said firmly. "This is far too serious for party talk. Let's go back inside and get some champagne. I think you're old enough to have one glass of bubbly."

After moving back into the flow of the party, she took the last glass of champagne off a waiter's tray and handed it to Tricia. Beth laughed as her daughter wrinkled her nose at the fizz.

"Hey, this tastes pretty good," she announced.

"Well, just sip it. It's not as innocent as it seems," Beth cautioned.

Beth introduced Tricia to the wives of two of the board members, all the while very aware of Jonathan's eyes continually watching her. Her skin felt as though he were caressing it. She wished everyone else in the huge room would vanish, leaving only Jonathan and her to be alone with each other, and that they did not have to play out this stupid charade, playacting that they were only acquaintances, that they weren't hopelessly in love.

Why "hopelessly?" Why did that word come to mind? Was it just an expression, or deep in her heart did she know that there were too many obstacles— from an insecure teenager to a fund drive for a multimillion-dollar research facility to her own identity crisis? And they had no money. Both she and Jonathan were without financial resources. Even time was against them. Jonathan had no time for courtship. His life for the next three years would not be his own. In fact, his life never would be his own. His responsibilities to others would always pull him away from her. And she was weary of the noble wife role.

But then, Jonathan had never promised her a future. They talked of everything but the future. There had been no talk of marriage. Not even any talk of love. Words of passion—yes, they shared much of that. They spoke of the joys of their lovemaking. Before they made love, they teased each other with words of their need. Afterward, with great fascination, they replayed their passion, telling each other in tantalizing detail how it had been for them.

But they did not pledge undying love. They did not talk of commitment and marriage. They did not discuss names for children.

Yet Beth felt a need for all those things. She wanted Jonathan's undying love. She wanted a commitment from him. And she wanted to have a baby with him.

But she was also afraid of what those things would bring if she had them. There was still the voice inside her that refused to be quiet. *Who are you?* it said. *Is love enough to offer a man? Shouldn't you also have a sense of self?* Without a sense of self, she feared that a marriage to another surgeon would be a repeat performance for her. She would be alone much of her life. She would slip into the shadows and lose herself again.

So for her and Jonathan the future was defined as the next time they would be together. And their words were of lovemaking, not of love. Perhaps the word "hopelessly" was apt. Beth thought of the popular song about "hangin' on until the good is gone." Was that what they were doing? And when the problems of being together overwhelmed the good, would they drift apart?

For herself, however, Beth feared the good would never be gone. She could not imagine a day she would not want to see Jonathan Sky. Or a night. She wanted him in her bed and in her life forever.

Her thoughts went around in circles so fast they made her dizzy.

Tricia had fallen into a conversation with the son of one of the board members—a medical student at Berkeley. It gave Beth the opportunity at last to cross the room to where Jonathan stood talking with two other residents. He saw her coming and detached himself from them while grabbing two champagne glasses from a passing waiter.

In spite of her pensive mood, Beth could not stop the smile from coming to her face. If anyone were observing her at this moment, she was certain her smile revealed what was in her heart. She was in love with that fantastic-looking man with the dark, brooding eyes. Just the sight of his hands grasping the stems of those two glasses was almost more than she could bear. Beautiful hands—strong, with long, tapering fingers that in another age would have drawn back an arrow in a bow to stalk his prey but instead used a surgeon's knife to attack disease. Beth thought his hands all the more wonderful because they had no hair to mar their perfection—only smooth, veined skin— like that on his smooth, muscled chest. Jonathan, like most Indian men, had very little body hair. To Beth, it added to his exotic beauty. She thought of her fingers caressing Jonathan's pure, sculptured chest. Oh, yes, if only she were doing that now. Her fingers ached to touch his flesh, to explore his fine masculine body.

Handing her a glass, Jonathan said softly, "You're gorgeous. I guess you know that every step you take drives me wild. I want to kiss that provocative thigh that peeks out at me. I want to kiss its hidden mate. I want to remove your blouse and kiss your breasts. I want to take off your shoes and kiss your insteps. I want to take off everything else so I can kiss every inch of your body. I'd kidnap you back to my apartment if I didn't have to do the emergency room in less than an hour. Can we get together tomorrow?"

"Oh, I hope so," Beth said, thinking of her own set of longings. Could she wait until tomorrow? Her need for this man had become an insatiable thing. It was forever with her. "Tricia's feeling very threatened by you. I may need to see how she's doing tomorrow. But yes, I'll try, my darling. I'll try."

Jonathan glanced at his watch. "I've got at least to kiss you before I leave here. I'll go upstairs as if I'm heading for the rest room. You follow in about two minutes; we can duck into one of the rooms."

"There's a rest room downstairs," Beth said teasingly. "Right across the hall."

"But I don't know that," Jonathan said with a wink. "See you in two minutes."

She wanted that, too—to kiss him, to feel his arms around her, if only for a moment.

She sipped her champagne and moved toward the edge of the room, not wanting anyone to engage her in conversation. She wasn't sure if two minutes had gone by yet, but she put down her glass and started for the foyer.

"Ah, Beth, there you are. I've been looking for you."

With a sinking heart, Beth turned to see Richard Ballard smiling at her. Always the dandy of the hospital staff, he was wearing a red shantung sport coat and white trousers. She returned his smile and frantically tried to think of something to say to get away from the surgeon. "I have a lover waiting upstairs" would not do. "I was just on my way to the powder room" she said. "Talk to you in a minute."

"Actually, I'm just leaving," he said, looking down at his diamond-studded watch. "Duty calls. But I just wanted to ask you how you're doing on the memoir project?"

"Just fine," Beth said. "I'm surprised you even know about it. I understood it was supposed to be kept under wraps until we had a publisher and could make a big public announcement."

"Well, I just found out about it this evening," Ballard admitted. "Betty Wishart mentioned it to me. Fine idea. If anyone deserves to be immortalized, it's Justin Dunning. It was a privilege to work with him all those years. I understand he kept very complete journals?"

"Yes, as a matter of fact he did. He wrote in them almost daily."

"Is that right? Incredible for a man that busy," the slender physician said, thrusting his hands into his pockets and striking a casual pose. "What a treasure of information he must have left. Have you read them all?"

"Yes, every one," Beth replied, wondering at the surgeon's curiosity. Keeping a journal wasn't so unusual.

"Really?" Ballard asked with a questioning lift of his eyebrows. "I suppose he mentions all of us who were serving at Healing Arts all those years along with him?"

"Of course," Beth said, wondering whether Ballard wanted to make sure he was included in the book or if he was afraid of something Justin might have written in his journals. "He has a lot to say about his association with you, for example."

"I'm sure he did," Ballard said smoothly. "Justin and I had a few problems over the years, but all in all we had an excellent professional relationship."

"Of course, he wrote far more than we can ever put in a book," Beth said, wondering how long Jonathan would wait upstairs before he gave up. How could she politely escape from this man? "It all makes very interesting reading. But I can assure you that nothing will be published that would reflect badly on the hospital or its medical staff.''

"Oh, so he does include some negative stuff in the journals,'' he said, reaching for a glass of champagne from a passing waiter. Beth's heart sank. Ballard had said he was on his way out the door, and now he had another drink.

"I'm not sure if you are aware of the power struggle that's beginning to take shape at Healing Arts,'' he continued. "If the wrong side wins, a lot of Justin's original concept for the center will be changed. I, for one, would hate to see that. If there is anything in those journals that might expose his enemies and give us some ammunition to prevent that from happening—well, needless to say, I'd like to know what it is.''

So she was being pumped for information, Beth realized with irritation. And she was being encouraged to take sides in Healing Arts internal squabbles.

"I'm aware that there had been problems at the center, but I'd be hard-pressed to pick sides, Richard,'' she said, glancing toward the stairs. "I'm sure Justin's original concept didn't include using hospital residents as pawns. They should be selected for their talent and their dedication and not by whose side they are on. And I understand that you and Christenson are both eager to have your own man as chief resident and not Dr. Sky, whom my husband had long ago identified as the most talented among the surgical residents. And now will you please excuse me? One of my contact lenses has slipped, and it's driving me crazy. Nice to talk to you.''

For effect, Beth blinked her right eye over the non-existent lens and scooted away, heading for the elegant staircase that curved itself around the most incredible crystal chandelier Beth had ever seen.

Her heart pounded as she headed up the stairs. What if Jonathan had given up on waiting for her? It was ridiculous how much she wanted a few minutes alone with him. Absolutely ridiculous. But she would have climbed a mountain for one of his kisses.

He was standing in the shadows at the far end of the hall. "In here," he said.

They ducked into a dark bedroom. Beth could see the corner of a canopied bed before Jonathan closed the door, surrounding them in darkness, and threw his arms around her.

"Beth, Beth," he said into her hair. "Oh, my God, Beth, I'm crazy about you. I think about you constantly. I want to be with you constantly."

His kiss was almost violent in its intensity. And Beth responded in kind. Again the feeling returned that they were trespassing in some otherworldly place— that mere mortals weren't allowed feelings like this. This was forbidden pleasure, unspeakable delight. When she was with him like this, she could forget everything else and melt in the heat of his passion.

But the kisses made her want more than kisses. She felt his arousal, and it only served to escalate her own need. Oh, how glorious it was to know that she affected him like that!

The bed was behind her. Could she be that wanton—to make love while a party was going on downstairs?

No, of course not.

What if Tricia came looking for her?

Tricia, Beth thought with a start. She had to get back downstairs to Tricia.

But just one more kiss. When Jonathan kissed her, he touched her soul. She had no idea a kiss could be so intimate, so giving, so full of promise, so filled with longing and love.

The sound of the door opening forced her abruptly back from passion. White light filled the room.

She heard Betty Wishart's gasp before Beth actually saw the woman.

Mrs. Wishart, her husband and Tricia were standing in the doorway. Behind them were Martin Morrison and two of the foundation's board members. To the rear stood the men's wives, straining to see the room.

"What the hell?" Jonathan demanded, his voice angry.

"How dare you!" Mrs. Wishart shrieked. "In this room of all rooms. How could you?"

In this room? Beth looked around at a vision of white-and-pink eyelet. Ruffles everywhere. Dolls. Stuffed animals. An enormous doll house. Tiny dishes set out for tea on a child-sized table. A pink gown laid out on the bed. Slippers beside the bed. The canopied bed with the covers turned back, waiting for the child who would never come again.

Beth understood now. It was Cynthia's room. She and Jonathan had been necking in the room belonging to the Wisharts' dead daughter. Mrs. Wishart had apparently brought Tricia and the others up to tour the shrine.

"This is unspeakable. A travesty," Betty Wishart wailed while her husband tried futilely to calm her. "How dare you violate my baby's room. My pure little Cynthia. How could you?"

She turned to Beth. "You! His wife! Dr. Dunning's wife carrying on like that—like a common tramp. It's disgusting."

"I don't think it's disgusting," Tricia said, her voice quavering but quite clear over Mrs. Wishart's whimpers. "My father's been dead for over a year, and my mother and Dr. Sky have fallen in love. I'm sure they didn't realize this was your daughter's room, Mrs. Wishart, but even if they had, what difference would it make? Would your daughter have thought two people kissing in her room was so awful?"

Beth left Jonathan's side and went to her daughter. "Thanks, honey," she said as she hugged the dear girl she had raised and learned to love as her own, her dead husband's most precious gift to her. "You'll never know how much what you just said means to me."

"Yeah, I think I do," Tricia said. "I think I'm just beginning to understand a lot of things. Let's go home."

Chapter Eleven

"Fortunately, we'll be able to hush things up, since no one who witnessed that little scenario last night was outside the hospital family," Martin told her from behind the expanse of his oversized desk. Beth could hear the ever-present sound of large machinery from outside Martin's window as work continued on the hospital. Men's voices yelled anxious directions as the long neck of a huge crane swung into view, an enormous slab of precast concrete dangling from its grasp like the helpless victim of some huge, prehistoric beast of prey.

"But I guess I don't need to tell you," Martin continued, his tone one that a person would use to chastise a naughty child, "that I and the others are extremely disappointed in you. Oh, Beth, how could you?"

Beth was tired of coming to this office. She felt like a child summoned to the principal's office.

"How could I?" Beth laughed, a harsh, cynical laugh that sounded as if it belonged to another person. Surely Beth Dunning would never laugh cynically. "It was quite easy. Dr. Sky is a very attractive man," Beth said flatly. "Surely you didn't think I was going to remain a celibate, grieving widow forever?"

"Some women do," Martin replied pointedly, "especially if they were married to someone as important as Justin Dunning. If you hadn't been married to him, you'd be a nobody."

"No, you're wrong, Martin. I was nobody before. Now I'm going to try being a person."

She watched as Martin picked up his letter opener and balanced it between his index fingers. The smile that teased his lips was condescending.

"Oh, so you're into *that*. A woman in search of self-actualization. Well, just how do you plan to become a person, Beth? Certainly not by marrying a penniless resident who will soon be without a residency program. He'll never be a cardiovascular surgeon."

Beth gasped. "You wouldn't! Not just because of that fiasco last night. Listen here, Martin, if you take his residency away from him, I won't play ball with the rest of the fund-raising drive. I'll publicly become a loose woman. I'll tarnish the Dunning image. I'll tell the world that the great doctor didn't leave his wife and daughter a dime. I'll make up stories about him. He's dead and will never know. But Jonathan Sky's not dead, and he has his whole life ahead of him. I won't have him sacrificed to the whim of that pitiful Wishart woman."

"It's not just her," Martin said impatiently. "Christenson would like his own man to be chief resident. So would Ballard. Externally, Beth, the hospital may belong to the Dunning legend. But internally there is a power struggle going on to see whose hospital this is. I don't intend to give up everything I've worked for at this point in my life."

"And you and Christenson have joined forces," Beth said, "to prevent a coup. Just like a corrupt government in some little Latin American country, you will do what needs to be done to squelch an uprising. And all that talk you gave me about keeping Justin's memory alive and carrying out his dream was just so much talk to keep me in line, wasn't it? I'm just a pawn in a power struggle."

"What goes on here is important, Beth. You can't deny that. Lives are saved every day, every hour. Suffering is alleviated. But all that doesn't go on in a vacuum. Hospitals, like all large institutions, are ultimately political. There has to be a hierarchy. Someone has to be in charge. And I am the only one left who was here at the beginning. Justin and I, we started Healing Arts. He was the spirit. I was the organizer. I have supported Justin in this dream since our medical-school days. He had a vision, but I made it happen. I've earned the right to captain the ship. When Justin was alive, everyone deferred to him. I was the chief administrator, but Justin chaired the board and called all the shots. Now I can be in complete control. I've earned the right," he repeated.

"And you'll sacrifice a brilliant young surgeon's career if necessary."

"Of course," Martin said smoothly. "And in spite of your threats, I don't think you'll do anything to damage Healing Arts or Justin's memory. Even if you no longer care about preserving the respectability and prestige of your widowhood, you wouldn't do that to Tricia or to Justin's mother or to the future of a worthy institution. We are all, finally, controlled by what is best for Healing Arts."

"But what about Jonathan Sky?"

"He can try to get on at some other thoracic program," Martin said with a shrug, "or he can go back to Oklahoma and be a medicine man in a tepee. I'm sorry about him, but it can't be helped. That's part of the price I pay for Christenson's support."

"You know Jonathan can't just waltz his way into another program at this late stage of the game. He needs to finish his residency at a prestigious program to get accepted in one of the few cardiovascular fellowships available. You know very well if you send him away from Healing Arts, he'll have to go begging to some lesser program to pick him up. And then what are his chances of getting a fellowship?"

"Beth, you're boring me. The man is outstanding, and some other program might pick him up. But around here Jonathan Sky is a dead issue. Obviously we can't keep both you and Dr. Sky around here. The Wisharts are adamant about that. What matters is Healing Arts, and you are far more important to Healing Arts than Jonathan Sky—important enough that we are willing to help you financially in order for you to maintain yourself in a manner befitting Justin's widow. But don't think you'll get any more financial help if you continue to sneak around in disgusting little trysts with resident physicians. I used to think you were mature beyond your years, and now I'm beginning to wonder. Run along, Beth, and for heaven's sake, behave yourself. I'll see you at the governor's reception on Sunday. Wear something widowlike—without slits in the skirt. And incidentally, that was a brilliant idea to bring Tricia last night. Why don't you bring her along on Sunday?"

Beth stood and looked down at the man who had been her husband's lifelong friend and supporter. "Go

to hell, Martin,'' she told him before she walked out
of the room.

BETH STARED OUT of the living room window at the
heavy sky and the restless sea. The palm trees that
lined the wall at the cliff's edge were bending and
swaying in response to the gusty wind. Dead fronds,
ripped from the trees, scurried across the back lawn
and found their way into the swimming pool. And inside the room the timeless voice of Nat King Cole
singing of blue velvet came from the stereo, his mel-
low tones contrasting with the building fury on the
other side of the windowed wall.

Another storm was predicted, with gale-force winds.
Beth was glad she hadn't cleaned the pool. It would
just have to be redone after the storm. When Jonathan got off the phone, she'd have him help her drag
the lawn furniture into the garage—if he had time,
that is.

She wondered if he was going to have to go back to
the hospital. He was not on first call, but the summons on his pager to call the hospital switchboard
could only mean a problem. That's the only kind of
summons physicians ever got. Problems. Unless re-
quested to do so, nurses never called to say a patient
was doing well. Once again, as she found herself doing
so often of late, Beth wrestled with her own problem.
She and Jonathan could not continue drifting along
with no discussion of what the future held for them.
She sensed that he was in the process of thinking
through his own set of problems concerning their relationship.

Two of the obstacles that stood in the way of her
making a commitment to Jonathan no longer both-

ered her. Beth realized that Tricia had come to terms
with the fact that her stepmother might someday re-
marry.

And Beth knew it was time to sever her ties with the
Healing Arts Medical Center. She realized now, after
her confrontation with Martin Morrison, that she
could not continue to put her life on hold in order to
fulfill Justin's unfinished dream. For one thing, the
dream no longer belonged to her dead husband, but to
whichever side would come out on top of the power
struggle that was erupting behind the scenes at the
medical center. Beth sensed that both sides considered her to be part of the spoils. Whoever won the
fight for control assumed that their founder's widow
would meekly support them as they built their empire. Well, if Healing Arts was as worthy and important as both sides claimed it was, then it could
certainly survive on its own merits and would not be
irreparably damaged if Beth gave up her widowhood
in favor of a new life. Amazing how obvious it all
seemed now that the agonizing was over and her decision made.

But did she want to make her life with another physician? If Jonathan worked out his own set of problems and came to her with words of love and marriage,
did she want her life dictated to by the inevitable radio pager clipped on her husband's belt, especially
when she happened to be deeply in love with that husband? Maybe she wasn't noble enough to be always
philosophical about it. Patients would always come
first. They had to. That was the nature of the profession.

But more than that, more than having to play second fiddle to patients and to the mightiest mistress of

them all—medicine—did she want once again to enter into marriage with a man who by virtue of his noble, highly respected and incredibly demanding profession so overshadowed his wife as to make her practically anonymous? If only she had finished college or done something worthwhile herself, maybe she wouldn't feel intimidated by a physician husband. If she were an attorney or owned a business or were artistic, if she were anything special, perhaps she would be more self-assured and would not slip once again into the shadows of a man who operated on people's hearts, who fought battles with death every day of his life.

But she wasn't special. The most special thing she had ever done was to have her life saved by a famous surgeon. Beth knew she had no talents, no achievements, no credentials. She had never been anything but a housewife. She had never had a job, never earned a dime. And she wasn't one of those women clever at organizing things. The only thing she had ever been particularly good at was mothering Tricia. Well, maybe two things. Since she no longer had a gardener, she discovered she definitely had a green thumb. But the only thing she had ever been known for was being the wife, and now the widow, of Justin Dunning. Without Justin, she had no identity at all.

No identity. No money. And soon no home, apparently.

She was petitioning the court now to release her from the terms of Justin's will and be allowed to sell the house. If she could sell it, she and Tricia would use what equity there was left to live on for a time. She just hoped permission would be given before the mortgage company foreclosed.

Beth didn't turn around as Jonathan came back into the room. She stared out at the twisting palm trees and waited for him to tell her about a patient or an emergency awaiting him. And she would have to smile and send him off. She couldn't whine about the beautiful fresh salmon steaks waiting to be broiled—an extravagance that she could ill afford but that she had bought in honor of this special evening. He was going to spend the night with her. They were to be alone—all night. Tricia had discreetly elected to spend the weekend with her grandmother to give them some privacy. Dear Tricia. Wisdom had come hard for her, but now that she had found it, she seemed to have grown up overnight. In fact, it was Tricia who had suggested Jonathan might want to sleep over. Imagine.

Beth could hear Jonathan at the bar. Beth wondered what he could possibly find to drink there. Scarcely anything was left of her liquor supply. Other than inexpensive wine, alcoholic beverages were an extravagance she had long since given up.

The cloying smell of crème de menthe greeted her nostrils. It had an almost nauseating effect on Beth.

"None for me," she said. "I don't even like it on ice cream."

"Nothing's the matter with your olfactory powers. Would a cup of tea smell better?"

"Sure," Beth said, and followed him into the kitchen. Actually, tea sounded good to her. Comforting.

She sat on the high kitchen stool and watched him make his way around her kitchen. Strange, how much it pleased her to see a man in her kitchen. He even cooked. Beth had never known a man who cooked.

He heated the water in the microwave. She wondered if he would remember her teaspoon of sugar. He did. And he remembered to get out the tin of tea biscuits.

She waited for him to tell her. They were calling out the surgery crew. He would have to be there inside the hour. Don't wait up. It would probably be late. Sorry about the salmon. Would it freeze? They could try again his next free evening.

But instead, he handed her the cup of tea and said softly, "My grandfather died."

"Oh, Jonathan, I'm so sorry," Beth said with a stab of guilt. His phone call hadn't been about a patient at all.

"No need to be sorry. He was a very old man and died peacefully and with dignity. I rejoice for him. He was an elder in our tribe and very respected. My family will gather for the funeral."

Jonathan stared out the window over the sink, his eyes distant. He had forgotten her and this house. He was in Oklahoma with them—with his people. Suddenly Beth felt very removed from him, sensing more strongly than ever before the differences in their backgrounds. It was yet another thing that separated them. First there was medicine; then his Indian heritage. Beth shivered involuntarily. She didn't like being separated from him physically—or in spirit, which was worse. She felt cold and alone. The tea did not warm her.

In such a short time, this man had become the focus of her life. That frightened her. By loving him, she had made herself vulnerable and open to pain. And there was so much that could keep them apart. After Justin died, she had vowed never again to depend on

a man for everything in her life. She craved the security that independence would bring. If one were independent, the world couldn't be pulled from beneath
one's feet because of a relationship that had too many
strikes against it ever to become permanent. Yet here
she was, already needing a man for comfort, wanting
very little out of life but to be with him. And if he left
her, she would be every bit as lost as she was when
Justin died. Worse. For she feared that she had already given Jonathan Sky her very soul.

Other than Tricia, Beth realized she had no focus in
her life but Jonathan. And Tricia would soon be
grown. Beth's vague dreams about a fulfilling career
were without any direction. She felt such a distance
between herself and the things that used to matter to
her—Healing Arts, this house, the various women's
organizations to which she belonged. Even that damn
swimming pool, which would soon be filling with the
storm's debris, used to be important to her.

Jonathan was important to her. She had no wish for
the future but to be with him. And that did indeed
make her vulnerable.

Even now the death of his grandfather meant only
one thing to her—that he might go away for a time.
How selfish she was. But she couldn't help herself. The
thought of being separated from him by half a continent was frightening. Panic rose in her breast? What
if he never came back? What if the pull of his roots
was too strong? Maybe he would realize his place was
back there, with an Indian wife at his side. Beth
thought of the mother of his son. Would she be there
too?

"Will you go back for the..." She paused. Was
funeral the correct word? She thought of pictures she

had seen of Indian burial customs—shrouded bodies high above the ground on wooden platforms. But no, that was long ago. "Will you go back to Oklahoma for his funeral?"

"I am the eldest grandson," Jonathan said, as though that was answer enough. "Come with me, Beth."

Beth wasn't sure that she had heard him correctly. Go with him to his grandfather's funeral?

He turned to face her, his gaze focused on her and not on some distant vision. "Come with me to Oklahoma," he said earnestly. "I want you to."

"But how?" Beth asked. "Neither one of us can afford the money for a plane ticket. And Tricia—"

"Tricia can stay on with her grandmother. Her school doesn't start for another week, so that will be no problem. And I'll borrow the money for the tickets."

"But I'm not family," Beth said hesitantly. "I'd feel strange and in the way."

"My family would be honored if a lovely lady such as yourself shared their hospitality. I wouldn't ask you, Beth, if it wasn't all right."

"And you really want me to go?"

By way of an answer, he took the cup of tea from her hand and placed it on the counter. He drew her into his arms, engulfed her with his embrace, surrounding her with his physical being. She felt warm and safe. The feel of him, the aroma of him, the taste of him, as she kissed him, the sound of him as he murmured words of longing—she was beyond help. Maybe she should not give her heart to this man. Maybe she should find herself before she loved again. Maybe she should hold back something of herself for safe keeping. She felt as if she were jumping out of an airplane without checking to see if she had a parachute on. But she was already sailing out the door of the plane. She was already on her way to disaster or ecstasy. It was too late to go back. She had either lost herself or found the world.

AS THE PLANE came out of the clouds over central Oklahoma, Beth eagerly looked out the window. Her initial response was disappointment. It was so flat. So very flat.

Jonathan's mother met them at the airport. Carlotta Sky was a slender woman whose black hair was peppered with the first showings of gray. Her cheekbones matched Jonathan's. But thanks to her mixed blood, her eyes were green. Carlotta's mother had been white.

As they drove southwest out of Oklahoma City, Beth saw that the land was indeed as flat as it had looked from the airplane. But as they drove from the town of Norman, with its skyline of university highrise dormitories and an enormous football stadium with a towering press box that dominated all else, and then headed west, the land took on a pleasant roll. Norman stood on the cross timbers, Jonathan explained. Eastern Oklahoma was wooded. West of Norman was prairie. And the prairie was his home. The Kiowa, Comanche, Cheyenne, Osage, Pawnee, Caddo, Arapaho and Wichita had hunted here, following the great buffalo herds that migrated from the north to graze on the prairie grasses. They were the Plains Indians and rode their ponies over the vast expanse—hunters who left little mark on the land, who

were one with nature. There was pride in his voice as
he told Beth what this land once meant to his people.

How far apart the towns were, Beth thought. It was
at least thirty minutes since they had left the community of Blanchard, with its two-block-long business
section that had not seen prosperity in many decades.
Along the coast of Southern California, the cities all
ran together; signs indicated when you left one and
entered the other. Not so in western Oklahoma; there
towns sat alone, isolated from one another like tiny
islands arising out of a sea of prairie grass.

Finally, however, they drove into Clearwater, a plain
little town dominated by two water towers and a grain
elevator. Its downtown was built around an aging
sandstone courthouse of nondescript architecture.
There were as many pickup trucks as cars parked
around the courthouse square. Many vehicles were
parked in the center of the wide street.

There was a World War I monument in the square.
Jonathan said the town never got around to erecting
one for World War II and simply stuck a second
"Honor Roll" plaque under the one honoring the
dead from the first war. And on the back side was a
smaller plaque for Korea. One for Vietnam was coming, he supposed. Things didn't move too fast in
Clearwater, however.

Old men sat around the square on park benches
shaded by elm trees, some whittling, some snoozing,
some just soaking up the sunlight.

No, Jonathan could not come back here, Beth
thought as she looked over the town. Without seeing
the hospital, she already knew Jonathan was vastly
overtrained for such a community. Somehow she had
assumed his home would be near a major city. Every-

place she herself had ever lived was in a metropolitan area. But Oklahoma City was 160 miles to the east, and Tulsa farther yet. There was no large city anyplace nearby. Highly specialized surgeons such as Jonathan could only work out of large medical centers with all the latest technology.

The days when Jonathan Sky could live in Clearwater ended years ago. Beth speculated that the town probably had two or three family doctors and a twenty-bed hospital. No more.

The home of Carlotta Sky was set to the back of an acreage on the edge of town. The frame house was in need of paint; but it was shaded by an enormous elm tree and had a charming, broad front porch that went around two sides of the building. A porch swing hung in the angle where the porch turned the corner. The leaded glass panes in the handsome front door spoke of grander times.

Inside, varnished hardwood floors were covered with handsome Indian rugs. But other than the rugs and the paintings by Jonathan's father that decorated the walls, the house was furnished conventionally. It was very pleasant, immaculately clean, and yet, the whole house could have fit into Beth's living room.

Beth met two of Jonathan's sisters and their offspring. The women and children looked at her with curious eyes, but their welcome was warm.

Very shortly, Beth, Jonathan and Carlotta went to visit Jonathan's grandmother. His grandparents' home, an even smaller house than the one in which Jonathan had grown up, was in the country.

To one side of the house was a huge vegetable garden. "The deer used to get in there and wreck the garden when I was a kid," Jonathan told her. "My cousins and I used to sleep on the porch in the summertime so we could watch for them and chase them away. We used to pretend that we were on the lookout for a renegade band of Sioux or the U.S. Cavalry. We devised our own version of 'counting coup'—that means chalking up a brave deed in battle—by pulling a tail feather out of one of my grandmother's roosters. I still have scars on my leg where a particularly valiant Rhode Island red got the best of me.''

They sat on lawn chairs under a brush arbor and drank ice tea with Grandmother Sky and two of Jonathan's aunts. The old woman's face was weathered and wrinkled, her long plaited hair completely gray. But her eyes were bright and alert. She was obviously delighted to see her grandson.

She asked Beth about her home and her daughter. "No Indian blood, I suppose," the old woman said matter-of-factly.

Beth shook her head no. She felt as if she should apologize for the oversight. Beth knew the old woman would have preferred that Jonathan bring someone of Indian blood home to meet his family.

Their tea finished, they went on to the funeral home.

The old woman, with a shawl around her shoulders, took her grandson's arm, and they went to pay their respects to the dead. Beth found it strange to see a man in death whom she had never known in life, and she kept to the back of the room, watching as the four women and tall young man stood by the casket, which was draped with a new Pendleton blanket rather than flowers.

"Tuesday he died," Grandmother Sky was saying in her raspy old woman's voice as the five of them stared down into the casket. "The wind blew all day on Monday, but Tuesday it was calm, and the sun was warm. He saw a red-tailed hawk circling in the sky. He had a good day to die. When he woke up that morning, he said, 'Old woman, today I will leave you.' And I told him, 'Not for long you won't, old man'."

Abruptly, she turned to her grandson. "Your grandfather said to tell you not to forget you are an Indian. He prayed for you before he died."

"Grandmother, I have never forgotten who I am."

"And he said that I should tell you always to examine your heart and know that you do what is right and not what other people have decided for you. Then we have only ourselves to blame or to thank for our actions."

"He spoke wisely," Jonathan said solemnly.

"He said that if you use an Indian's wisdom along with white man's science, you will be a good healer of men. He said that doctors and all men must be humble before nature. You must not forget to renew your spirit each day in contemplation, with only the sky over your head and the earth under your feet."

"I will remember his words," Jonathan promised.

"We put moccasins on his feet," one of the aunts said. "He will walk as an Indian in the Other World."

They went from the funeral home to a prayer service at the rustic Native American church that was located several miles from town in a glade between two high red bluffs. Before the service began, Jonathan and Beth climbed to the top of the higher bluff to watch the sunset. The vast prairie, dotted with occasional farmhouses and a few broken-down windmills, stretched out in front of her for mile after endless mile. The unbelievably vivid sunset filled the western sky.

"They say that in the old days when the buffalo migrated," Jonathan told her, "the herd stretched from here to the horizon, that it was buffalo as far as the eye could see."

"You love this land, don't you?" Beth asked. The slanting rays of the setting sun accentuated the contours of his strong face. There was a rightness about being here with him.

"Yes. I forget sometimes just how much. In the operating room, it's easy to forget everything else. You're so focused on the life there on the table that who people are and where they came from simply don't matter. And that's good. But at other times one does need to remember, to come back, to stand here and get in touch with the bigger picture."

He looked out across the land, seeing his private visions. "I used to come here with my grandfather," he said, his words as much for himself as Beth. "We would sit on that flat rock over there, and he would tell me stories of the old days and of his own grandfather. And my cousins and I would come out here and look for arrowheads. When we were kids, you could still find them. I guess if I had to pick one spot on the earth that was my spiritual center, it would be this red bluff."

"Thank you for sharing this place with me," she told him. "It's so beautiful, and I feel so peaceful—it's almost as though I've been here before."

"You have," he said, his face breaking into a broad grin. "In my dreams. We made love right here on the top of the bluff."

Jonathan took her into his arms and kissed her. He seemed to sense that it was tenderness she needed and not passion. He held her for a long time.

The funeral was held the next day, and the old man was laid to rest in the Native American cemetery. While his casket was lowered into the ground, a young man softly beat a hand drum; those assembled sang songs in the ancient language. The blanket from the top of the casket was presented to Jonathan.

Afterward the clan gathered at Carlotta's house. Makeshift tables consisting of sawhorses and planks were grouped around the huge old elm tree. Women from the church laid out the food, and everyone sat for hours in the shade of the old tree, renewing family ties and remembering the ones who had gone beyond.

"When Grandmother goes, there will be no one left of that generation," Jonathan realized as he looked around the gathering of his kinfolk. "Funny, I thought we would always have those ancient ones among us to keep the old ways alive. I guess as each generation dies out, the next has to take up the torch."

"Someday it will be your job," Beth said, knowing that she was stating his own thoughts. She understood that he would always return to this place for the funerals, the weddings, the powwows. Already they were planning a memorial powwow for Jonathan's grandfather to be held one year from the day he died. There would be a part of Jonathan that always belonged to this world, a world she could never share—just as she could never share his surgeon's world. She now realized how little she and Justin had shared during their marriage. Even Tricia. For the girl had become more Beth's than Justin's. Beth had raised Tricia by herself. She had kept the house and waited, always waited, for the busy man to come home, for his perfunctory kisses, for serving him a meal before he rushed back to emergencies and meetings or off to bed because he had an early case in the morning.

Beth wrapped her arms around herself and hugged her body as though attempting to alleviate the wave of loneliness that washed over her.

She watched Jonathan move among his relatives. She saw the respect they had for him, this clansman of theirs who had made them all proud. Already it seemed as if they looked to him for leadership.

Carlotta brought Beth some hot coffee and just-cooked fry bread. "It's tasty but heavy on the stomach of the uninitiated," she warned.

Beth sipped the coffee and nibbled at the traditional Indian bread. It was quite good. But after a while she found it did indeed sit heavy on her stomach, and so she gave the uneaten portion to a yellow dog of uncertain parentage.

Later, she and Jonathan took Grandmother Sky back to the cemetery and left her there by the mound of fresh dirt to bid her private farewell to the man with whom she had lived her life. Once again Jonathan and Beth climbed the bluff, the old woman's keening following them up the hill.

"I wondered if she would get to crying," Beth said. "She seemed so reconciled to it all."

"She will be very lonely without him," Jonathan said. "In the old days, she would have been required to make some public display of grief, like cutting off her hair or even a finger. Some of the old ways were easier to let go than others."

Beth thought how lucky Jonathan's grandmother and grandfather had been to have each other all those years. She could tell from the way the old woman talked about her husband of more than fifty years that she had loved and respected him and that he must have felt the same about her in return. What more could people ask of life than to share it with a soul mate?

Jonathan drew her to his side, and arm in arm they stood in this special place. Beth felt better than she had all day. She liked it here with him, but already a part of her was leaving this place and moving on into tomorrow, to the return flight home, to the problems that awaited her there. Would the court allow her to sell the house? Where would she and Tricia live? And what would she do with the rest of her life? And Jonathan. Would she someday look back on these moments with him on the high bluff in Oklahoma and wonder whatever happened to the beautiful Indian surgeon whom she had loved so completely? Maybe as his fame grew, she would read about him from time to time in the pages of some newspaper or magazine. And she would stare at a picture of an older but still handsome Dr. Sky. She would touch the picture with her fingertips, and she would weep for what might have been.

For she had no illusions. She knew if she did not have Jonathan for the rest of her life, she would miss him every single day. Thoughts of him would never leave her. She had never understood love and passion before Jonathan. She never understood how crippling it could be. For without this man she could never be whole again.

Jonathan cared for her. Beth knew that. But he had never spoken of a future for them. She realized he knew very well the obstacles that lay in their path. She also sensed that this trip to Oklahoma had created another one. He would probably return to the Southwest someday—not to little Clearwater but to some city in this region. The pull of family and tribe was too strong. And what if he felt the need to share his life with someone whose background was similar to his own?

Beth was so tired of the continuous turmoil that went on in her mind. She was bored with perpetual problems. She was ready for peace.

So for these moments at least she put those problems out of her mind and relished her time on the red Oklahoma bluff with this very special man. If this was all, she was damned lucky to have had this much. Without Jonathan, she might have lived her entire life never knowing what it truly was like to love a man.

She thought of a line of poetry. Was it from Emerson? No, she decided it was Tennyson who wrote, "'Tis better to have loved and lost than never to have loved at all."

How lucky she was, Beth thought as she leaned her head against his shoulder. She hoped they would make love tonight. Privacy was a problem with all the relatives around. Maybe they could come back here after they took his grandmother home. Yes, that would be wonderful. He said he had dreamed of making love to her on this high bluff. Maybe if she could make his dream come true, he could do the same for her.

Chapter Twelve

Beth took the university catalog from San Diego State
out of her desk drawer and carried it with her out to
the terrace. She had already pored over it so many
times that the catalog's pages were curled. But still she
searched. She still had the feeling that the answer to
her dilemma was written someplace on those pages, if
she were just clever enough to find it. It seemed that
all those novels she had read about women emerging
into a new life had them finding themselves on college campuses.

She sat thumbing through the catalog pages, waiting for inspiration to strike. Somewhere on these pages
there had to be an answer.

After a time however, she let the book drop into her
lap and stared out at the ocean. Two ships far out on
the horizon looked like a child's bathtub toys. There
was a slight haze in the air that gave the water a gray-
ish-green cast. But the day was warm and the ever-
moving sea calm.

The sea had been her constant companion for ten
years. She wondered what it would be like not to live
in this house, not always to have this view to greet her

each day. The ocean was so humbling, Beth thought, so intimidating, so awesome.

She thought of the rippling waves through the Oklahoma prairie grasses. She thought of the cottonwood trees along the creek banks and the hawks circling high in the incredibly blue, unpolluted sky. Somehow she had not felt so small and insignificant in Oklahoma. Except for the blue of the sky, nothing was awesome there. The beauty of the land was more subtle, more understandable.

And it was part of Jonathan. She felt something akin to homesickness for the land of his birth. Or was it only her longing to go where Jonathan would go? She didn't think he would remain in California.

But would life in Oklahoma really be any different? She would probably face the same problems there. Just moving to a different state didn't solve one's identity problems.

Beth picked up the catalog and held it at arm's distance. Maybe she should open it at random and with her eyes closed select what she should do for the rest of her life. She'd heard of people using that method to find answers in their Bibles. Beth picked up the book and without looking let it fall open. Then she closed her eyes, and jabbed at the page with her finger.

She opened her eyes and moved her finger to one side.

Drama. Her finger had landed in the middle of the class listing for the School of Drama.

At another time she would have laughed. It should be funny, but somehow it wasn't. A career in the theater. She'd never acted in anything in her life. And furthermore, she'd never really wanted to. Maybe no matter where she had jabbed her finger, she would have had the same feeling. A joke. She did not feel compelled toward any particular field of study. She would just like to skip around the schedule, taking classes in literature, perhaps, and French and botany and art appreciation, and learn to play the piano. Even archaeology. She had always wanted to know about that. However, she didn't want to spend the rest of her life in trenches at excavation sites. But she needed to focus on something, to prepare herself for a career. She wanted to make something of herself in order to be worthy of Jonathan. He deserved more than an anonymous woman standing quietly at his side. She didn't want to be cropped out of any more photographs. Jonathan deserved someone special. He deserved someone who would not be so overshadowed by him and his career that she became invisible. How could a man love someone who was invisible?

TRICIA ANSWERED the door.

"How's school?" he asked.

"A drag. Think you could find time to help me with my chemistry next weekend?"

"You bet. You may have to come down to the hospital, but we'll work something out. Where's your mother?"

"I think she's out back," the teenager called out to Jonathan as she slammed the front door and raced to answer the telephone.

Jonathan felt good about his relationship with Tricia. After sullen hostility, she had entered a stage in which she went out of her way to be nice and make small talk. Now she simply accepted his being there. No big deal. That was good, Jonathan realized.

He went through the kitchen, stopping at the refrigerator for a beer. He took two in case Beth also wanted one.

She was sitting on the terrace under the beach umbrella—crying. At first he wanted to rush to her, to comfort away whatever pain or problem she faced. But he held back. She seemed withdrawn. She needed the kind of comfort that comes from inside.

"I've heard of crying over a sad story—but a college catalog?" he said, indicating the book she held in her lap as he sat down beside her.

"I need to major in something," she said without looking at him.

"Oh?" he said gently. "I wasn't aware you were planning on earning a college degree."

"I have to," she said, wiping away her tears with the back of her hand. "It's the only way."

"The only way to what?" He placed the beer can in her hand and watched her take a long draft.

"To be somebody," she said with a shrug, as though the answer were self-evident.

"I thought you were somebody," Jonathan said, aching to pull her onto his lap, to kiss away her misery. But such behavior on his part would only compound what she was feeling.

"You know what I mean, Jonathan," she said, her tone one of irritation now. The tears were abating.

"No, I'm not sure I do," he said earnestly. "Do you think you could explain to me why the woman I love is nobody."

"You love me?" she asked. "Really?"

"With all my heart."

"Why didn't you tell me before?" she asked.

"Why have you never told me?" he retorted. "We both knew but felt so unsure. At first I was unsure because of your being the widow of Justin Dunning. That just blew me away. I thought I was into some unhealthy kind of quest to be the next Justin Dunning, right down to marrying his wife. But I worked through that in pretty short order. I realized I would have loved you if you were the widow of an ax murderer. Who you were married to didn't have anything to do with how I feel about you."

Jonathan waited a minute, letting her digest what he had said. He took a swallow of beer.

"Then I felt that I didn't have the time or the money to get involved with anyone," he continued. "And getting involved is distracting. I firmly believed that I needed all my time and money and concentration for the task at hand—making a cardiovascular surgeon out of myself."

"What changed your mind?" Beth wanted to know, her brown eyes wide and curious.

"Justin Dunning."

"What do you mean?" Beth asked, two little vertical lines creasing her smooth brow.

"Yeah, old Justin has been talking to me a lot here lately—through his journals and those letters people wrote to him, through you as I learn the kind of marriage you had with him, even through Tricia when we roasted wieners down on the beach the other night and I realized she had never done that with her father, never even once. He really didn't have any friends, only colleagues. He didn't allow himself any passion outside of medicine—not even for his intelligent, caring wife or his wonderful sweet daughter. He gave up so damned much to achieve what he did. I'm not sure it was worth it."

"But what about the good he did—all the lives he saved? Healing Arts itself?"

"Yeah. I kept asking myself that, too. He cut himself off from the full range of human experiences, but look at what he accomplished. So does that make it all right never to roast wieners with your daughter? I think not, Beth. I think there has to be a middle ground. I refuse to believe that people have to give their total lives to medicine like nuns and priests give their lives to the church. Justin could have shared some of his authority and responsibility with others. But he set himself up as some sort of a supersurgeon. And judging from the carefully written record he left, I rather imagine he jealously guarded his kingdom from any insurgents. What about vacations, for example? Think of the precious few times he took you and Tricia on a vacation. He was afraid to leave the kingdom he had created. He might miss out on making a miracle if he left."

"And you're not going to be like that?" Beth said, her eyes wide—those beautiful brown eyes that filled him with wonder.

"No, Beth, my darling, I will never build a research hospital to leave as a monument to my own greatness, like some pyramid built by an Egyptian pharaoh as a futile attempt at immortality. Oh, now don't say it," Jonathan said, holding up his hand in protest to the words she was about to utter. "Of course, Justin's 'monument' does a hell of a lot of good. But I'm talking about his motivation. I think Justin was building a pyramid to himself more than he was a hospital for the sick."

Jonathan reached for her hand. "I understand they used to seal servants up in the pyramids to serve the old guy in the hereafter. Well, times haven't changed so much. You're being walled up inside the Dunning pyramid. No wonder you feel out of touch with yourself and afraid. You're not being allowed to grow and change. You're being buried alive."

"Yes, but with Healing Arts I had a direction. Without it, what can I be? Who am I?"

Jonathan picked up the college bulletin from her lap.

"Is that what this is all about? A search for career and identity?"

Beth nodded.

"And you're worried that if you don't have a career and an identity outside of being the widow of Justin Dunning, then if you married me—a man pursuing a career similar to his—you'd be jumping out of the frying pan into the fire, so to speak? More of the same?"

Beth nodded, the misery returning to her face. "I was always overshadowed by him. I felt as if my life was absorbed by him. I didn't mind providing an orderly home for him and raising Tricia and doing the social bit and the volunteer stuff. But I never did anything just for me. I think it might have made a difference in my marriage if I had. Justin didn't take much notice of me, but then what was there to notice? I never did anything to earn his respect. I want to make myself over, but now I don't even know what I would do if I had the opportunity."

The tears began again.

"Beth, look at me."

She shook her head no. She didn't want to look at him. Beth looked out over the ocean, at the relentless sea he knew was disquieting to her at times, even after all these years of living at its edge. She told him once that she didn't mind the ocean when he was at her side. He wanted to be at her side forever, to bring her comfort for a lifetime. But in order to do that, she had to meet him halfway. If she fell into the same old traps, their life together would be doomed before it began.

He reached over and took her chin. He forced her to look at him.

"I am not Justin Dunning," he said almost ferociously. "A marriage to me would not be a repeat performance. It would be a new and original production. I may be a heart surgeon someday, but for God's sake, Beth, that doesn't make me a clone of Justin. I don't want the kind of life he wanted. I don't want to live in a showplace. I don't need to entertain the 'right' people because I'm not trying to build a damned empire. And our marriage would be the core of my existence. I would love you no matter what you did. You can go back to college if you want. I think you probably will want to do that someday. And you can work and have a career, or you can not work and be careerless. That doesn't have to be decided now. If you decide what you really want to do is stay home and raise vegetables or children or pigeons, that's okay, too. I'd prefer kids, but that's for us both to decide. I swear to you, Beth, that I want you to do whatever you need to do to grow and learn and feel good about yourself. We'll grow together. We'll travel and share books and music. I value your insights, your opinions, your curiosity. Don't ever think that I won't respect you. My

God, you are the most sensitive, loving woman I've ever known. I treasure you, Beth, and I promise ours will be a different sort of marriage. If you can't understand that, then by God, I don't want to marry you."

Jonathan abruptly pushed his chair back and walked to the edge of the terrace. The sea air assaulted his nostrils and gave him something to think about other than his pounding heart. He heard her footsteps. She was standing behind him.

"What will you do if they don't give you the chief residency?" she said softly.

"They've already given it to Clark Muldowny," he said without turning around. "But they'll let me finish out my residency at Healing Arts. Believe it ot not, Martin Morrison convinced the Wisharts I should be allowed to finish. Apparently he told them a bunch of stuff about not being able to document 'just cause' for dismissal and possible legal ramifications if I might sue the hospital. I may transfer or I may stay. I'm not sure. And what then? Well, I've been thinking about that. If the truth were known, I can probably get a fellowship someplace else."

"But I thought—"

"Oh, if you get passed over for a chief residency, it's much harder to get one of the best fellowships. But I have something in my favor. I'm an Indian."

Jonathan turned and sat on the terrace wall. He patted the wall next to him, and Beth sat beside him.

"I swore I'd never use my Indian blood to obtain special consideration," he said, taking her hand in his. "I wanted to make my way in the world without resorting to government quotas or being the token minority. But sometimes special circumstances make you eat your words. The fact of the matter is, I think there'll always be a prestigious program that would like a real, honest-to-God American Indian to add a colorful minority to its program and please their affirmative-action officer, provided, of course, I promise not to scalp any colleagues or build my tepee on the hospital grounds. Or maybe I'll settle for thoracic surgery and forget about going into cardiovascular. Maybe I'm not cut out to be the king of the mountain. Somehow I don't feel I have as much to prove as I used to. I know I could complete a cardiovascular program and be a competent heart surgeon. I don't have to prove it to myself anymore. And I've come to realize that what I feel inside is far more important than what other people think.''

"The future is very unsettled, isn't it?" She drew his hand up to her face and rubbed the back of it against her cheek.

"Very," Jonathan said, watching as she kissed his fingers one by one. "I don't know where we'll live. I admit I have strong yearnings to return to the Southwest, but who knows? We would have Tricia to consider. And I'd like to establish a relationship with my little boy in Oklahoma, if his mother will allow it. I don't know how we'll feed ourselves. I don't know anything except I love you and I want to spend the rest of my life with you. If we have each other, I don't mind uncertainties. Somehow we'll manage."

"It won't bother you if I don't wear proper little navy-blue dresses?"

"I'll introduce you as my mother if you do."

"And I don't have to belong to ladies' clubs and go to teas?"

"Not unless you want to."

Beth looked into his dark eyes with their heavy brows. "But I'm afraid you might someday regret the fact that you hadn't married an Indian woman and had children who were just as Indian as you are."

Jonathan shook his head in disbelief. "I fell in love with you. People can't decide to only fall in love with certain kinds of people. That would be about as superficial as deciding only to fall in love with rich people or blue-eyed blondes. Yes, I feel my roots deeply these days. But in my heart of hearts, I'm simply a generic man in love with a beautiful generic woman. As my grandfather counseled, I followed my heart. Sure, my family would have been pleased if I'd married an Indian woman, but it's not essential."

He traced the outline of her lips with his fingertip. He loved her completely—emotionally, spiritually and physically. Did she not understand how it was with them? "Beth, some things are just meant to be," he told her.

"And you won't think less of me if I don't know what I want to be when I grow up, even at age thirty?" Beth asked.

"At age thirty. Or forty. Or fifty. Maybe I'll retire in twenty years and let you support me if you do opt for a late-in-life career. In fact, you'll probably have a career of sorts right now, waiting tables or something of the like to help feed us. Is there anything else you want to clear up before we make this thing official?"

She nodded her head. Yes, there was something else.

"It's about birth control," she said, returning his hand to his own lap and avoiding his eyes.

"Yeah," he agreed. "We need to work something out better than the over-the-counter variety."

"It's too late." Her voice was a tiny whisper.

"You mean . . ."

Beth nodded. "That afternoon down on the beach. You didn't have anything then, and—well, I'm pregnant."

Jonathan thought of all the reasons he should be appalled by her news. His carefully made plans of how his life was going to be lived had all come crumbling down around his ears. He had no guaranteed fellowship waiting for him. He wasn't going to be chief resident. He was in love with a woman and wanted to get married years before he intended to. The woman was without financial resources and had a teenage daughter. And now she was pregnant. He was going to be a father—this time of a child he would be responsible for. He had no money and uncertain prospects. He'd be in hock up to his earlobes before he ever entered practice. But somehow it really didn't matter. A lot of what he had once thought important didn't matter anymore. They'd get by. Struggling residents and their families had done it before.

All that was important was that he and Beth be together. It was really so simple, and they had been making it so difficult .

"Guess that wraps you up as a fund-raiser for Healing Arts," he told her.

Beth nodded. "Guess it does. Martin will be horrified."

"Pregnant," Jonathan said with a shake of his head. "A baby. You're too much, lady."

"No," Beth corrected. "We're too much. It takes two to make a baby."

Jonathan anticipated her words and completed the last sentence with her. "It takes two to make a baby." Then he stood up abruptly and pulled her to her feet. With her hand firmly in his, he headed for the stairs to the beach.

"Where are we going?" Beth asked.

"To the scene of the crime," he said. "I want a reenactment."

Beth smiled, then threw her head back and laughed.

I'll remember the way she looks at this minute for the rest of my life, Jonathan realized as he took in her sparkling eyes, her windblown hair, the look of pure happiness on her beautiful face. *When I first saw her, I wanted to take the sad look from her eyes and bring laughter to her lips.* And he silently thanked the forces that had brought this moment to pass.

How long had he loved her? From the day of her husband's funeral? Or even before?

"I feel like I've loved you all my life," he told her.

Beth nodded. She understood. "And I love you, Jonathan Sky. I always will."

They hurried down the cliff's steep steps, and like two children, they raced hand in hand along the beach, their spirits high, their joy overflowing.

Their laughter blended with the call of the gulls. Jonathan turned a cartwheel. Beth turned two. They kicked their feet out of their shoes and played tag with the waves.

And they ran with the wind at their backs, the salt spray in their faces. They ran because they were in love and were young and happy and their baby grew within her. They ran because they had cut through the chains of the past and were free to make a future together.

When they came to their secret place among the marsh grasses, they knelt and grew suddenly quiet.

In the years to follow, both would look back at that time on the beach as their wedding. The other ceremony, the following week in a chapel, was for the benefit of Tricia, friends and colleagues.

But that day on the beach, they celebrated with their own ceremony.

Their laughter was past. Looking deep into each other's eyes, they pledged their love forever. By all that they held sacred, they made their promises. And with the words spoken, the tears of wonder shed, they made love.

Epilogue

"I want you to fill each one of the pots with dirt—all the way to the top," Beth told Amy. "Then we'll plant the seeds in them. And pretty soon little baby plants will grow."

Amy looked up at her mother with solemn brown eyes. Her short, dark hair was damp against her forehead. It was already hot in the greenhouse. Beth did most of her work here early in the morning, before the Oklahoma summer sun turned the greenhouse into a sauna. "Can I keep one for my very own?" she asked.

"Sure. We can make this corner shelf be just for Amy's plants."

Amy nodded eagerly. She liked that idea.

Then, with great seriousness, the three-year-old knelt down by the bin of soft humus and began filling the tiny red clay pots. Beth took a minute to relish the pure, innocent line of her daughter's neck as the child bent intently over her task. Beth leaned over to kiss the moist, sweet skin. How incredibly wonderful that such a small act as kissing the back of her child's neck could be so satisfying.

"When we finish with our work in the greenhouse, we have to get cleaned up and go to the grocery store,"

Beth said. "Do you remember what we have to do this afternoon?"

"Make a birthday cake for Tricia," Amy said, her face breaking into a happy grin. "Chocolate with white icing. And nineteen candles. And little silver candies sprinkled on top. Can I give her a baby flower in a pot for a present?"

"The seeds won't have sprouted by tonight," Beth explained, "but why don't you draw her a picture of a baby flower. I think she'd like that. And write your name at the bottom of it. Tricia doesn't know you can write your name. I'll bet she'll really be surprised! She can put the picture up on the bulletin board in her dormitory room. And she'll tell her friends that her smart little sister drew it for her."

Amy nodded. Yes, she would do that. She would color a picture and labor over an oversized, misshapened but legible A-M-Y.

Beth hoped Jonathan wouldn't be late this evening for Tricia's party. She was bringing four of her college friends from Norman home for dinner, and Beth had asked some of Tricia's friends from her high school days to stop by for cake and ice cream. But if Jonathan was late, they would not let it put a damper on the celebration. Beth knew that he wanted to be here with them and would come as soon as he could.

And they would have him all to themselves for two glorious weeks next month when they went to Colorado for their vacation. They had enjoyed the little mountain cabin so much last winter, they decided to go back and enjoy a summertime mountain vacation, too.

It was easier for Beth to get away now that she had one of her neighbors helping in the backyard greenhouse that she and Jonathan had built last year almost totally by themselves. The greenhouse had, to her astonishment, turned into a thriving neighborhood business. She had even accepted a couple of small landscaping assignments. She had been driving down to Norman three afternoons a week to take some landscape architecture courses at the university. She would take next semester off, however, for the birth of her second baby. She hoped to have enough time before the baby arrived to do some articles for the home-and-garden section of the Sunday supplement to the Oklahoma City newspaper—something she had been doing more and more of the past year. After she and Jonathan had completed the book on Justin's life, Beth found she missed working with words, and at Jonathan's encouragement she had attempted the first of her "Gardening with Beth" articles.

Already she and Jonathan were looking for an acreage on which they could build a home and a larger greenhouse so that she could start a plant nursery. They had decided to build a log home—roomy but rustic and homey. However, they were going to wait on that until they made a decision about Houston. They might be buying an acreage there instead. Jonathan had been offered a research fellowship at Baylor Medical Center in Houston. They must decide soon whether or not he should accept or continue as a thoracic surgeon at the University of Oklahoma Health Sciences Center in Oklahoma City.

They had gone to Houston last month for his interview. Beth liked the city with its lush vegetation and tall pine trees. Anything would grow in Houston. In Oklahoma, plants had to be tough enough to withstand extremes of temperature and frequent windstorms. In a way, however, she liked the challenge of Oklahoma. Except for the pine trees, Houston reminded her of Southern California. Tropical plants did not attract her as much as the hardier vegetation of the Great Plains. But each region had its own flora, its own particular beauty. And unless they lived at the South Pole, she could create beauty with her plants. She had a talent. She had discovered that while taking care of the yard in San Diego after financial necessity forced her to let the gardener go. Beth had read that adversity often helps people find their strengths. That had been true for her. She had discovered the joy of growing things, the pleasure of getting up each morning, and with the dew still on the leaves, checking on the progress of her garden, of doing a little pruning and incidental weeding before breakfast.

Gardening had taught her patience. She had become a creature not of days but of seasons, just like her plants. If one season was harsh, there was the promise of a kinder one to come.

She knew Jonathan was tempted by the Houston offer. He felt drawn more and more into the research arena. Whether in Oklahoma City or in Houston, he wanted to investigate the hereditary and cultural factors associated with heart disease. And the training he would receive at the prestigious Houston center would be fantastic. He seemed to have no regrets over his decision not to pursue a cardiovascular fellowship. He had decided, with the help of insights gained from working on Justin's book, that he wanted a more fully rounded life—one that left him more time for family and friends and tribal interests. He had allowed himself a year or two before making his final decision, but now he sincerely believed his professional contribution could best be made in the research arena where in the long run he could help far more people by pursuing new knowledge than by operating on individual patients.

With the money Beth received from the book project, they made a down payment on their present home. How ironic, Beth thought, that money from a book on her first husband's life had allowed her to begin life with a second. But life offers strange turnings.

Her first marriage had given her so much. Tricia. Self-knowledge. Health. The opportunity to be a part of the life of a very special man.

The court had allowed Beth to sell the San Diego house and put the money realized into a trust fund for Tricia. Beth severed her ties with Healing Arts but encouraged Tricia to represent her father at special occasions such as ground breakings and dedications.

But after the death of her grandmother Tricia's trips back to San Diego became less and less frequent. Like Beth, she now felt her home was here in Oklahoma.

And Jonathan liked living in Oklahoma. He was taking more responsibility in tribal affairs and even assuming a spokesperson role at times. He had been on television only last week, speaking against the proposed closing of the Indian hospital in Lawton, where he often volunteered his services. Amy had been astounded to see her daddy on a TV news program.

Carlotta Sky had made Amy, her youngest grandchild, a beautiful buckskin dress to wear to the powwows the family attended together in the summertime. And for Beth, Carlotta had made a fringed shawl to wear during the circle dances. Beth would never feel like an Indian, but having a part-Indian daughter helped her feel more at home when she attended a tribal or family gathering.

Beth would prefer to remain in Oklahoma where her husband's roots ran so deep, where her children, too, would know they belonged. But she knew that as long as she had her family and a growing season, she could find happiness.

The birthday cake was lopsided. And Amy's decoration of nineteen candles had a rather random arrangement. The top of the cake was generously covered with little silver candies. Tricia proclaimed that it was the best birthday cake she had ever had. She held Amy on her lap while together they opened the presents. Tricia's friends clustered about, laughing and joking with one another. Of the four friends who had accompanied Tricia from Norman, one was an earnest young man who looked at Tricia in a very special way.

Jonathan arrived just after the blowing out of the candles. Amy insisted that they light them again and repeat the singing of the happy birthday song. And this time she helped Tricia blow out the candles.

Jonathan's gift for Tricia was the most beautiful turquoise necklace any of them had ever seen. "One of my uncles made it," Jonathan told her.

Beth looked at the three of them—Amy still firmly enthroned on her big sister's lap, Jonathan kneeling beside them, his arm resting across Tricia's shoulders. Three heads leaned over the beautiful Indian necklace. Tricia's blond hair contrasted with two heads so dark the hair had a bluish cast. There was a beautiful naturalness about them clustered together. What a precious gift that the three people she loved most in the world also loved each other.

Beth's hand went to her still-flat tummy.

Was it her imagination, or had the baby in her womb stirred? Probably not. It was early for that.

But then she felt it again.

Welcome, small one, Beth thought. *I'm glad you could join us for this day.*

Jonathan looked up and smiled at her. Then he reached out and took her hand, linking them all together. A family.

"I love you," she whispered.

Jonathan didn't hear her for Amy's chattering. But it didn't matter. He already knew.

Harlequin American Romance

COMING NEXT MONTH

173 WELCOME THE MORNING by Bobby Hutchinson

To Charlie Cossini and her construction crew, work came first, even when the job site was in sunny Hawaii. So when surfer playboy Ben Gilmour wanted her for a playmate, he was forced to devise a plan to lure Charlie away form her hammers and lathes . . . and into his arms.

174 THE RUNAWAY HEART by Clare Richmond

Barbara Emerson should have been suspicious of a man as elusive as private investigator Daniel McGuinn, but instead she hired him to find a missing person. Sometimes, she thought, you had to gamble on blind instinct and hope that your instincts were right.

175 SHOOTING STAR by Barbara Bretton

To staid Bostonian Katie Powers, the advice "Be daring" was difficult to follow. Until she was stranded in a tiny Japanese village with fellow American Tom Sagan. Then the unexpected happened: over a spectacular display of fireworks, Katie fell in love.

176 THE MALLORY TOUCH by Muriel Jensen

Randy Stanton didn't think much of Matt's famed "Midas touch." Though he brought prosperity to the quaint Oregon coastal town, whenever they were together disaster followed close behind. But try as she might to avoid him, it seemed fate had set them on some kind of bizarre collision course.

ATTRACTIVE, SPACE SAVING BOOK RACK

Display your most prized novels on this handsome and sturdy book rack. The hand-rubbed walnut finish will blend into your library decor with quiet elegance, providing a practical organizer for your favorite hard-or-soft-covered books.

Only $9.95

Approximately 16" x 8" when assembled

Assembles in seconds!

To order, rush your name, address and zip code, along with a check or money order for $10.70 ($9.95 plus 75¢ postage and handling) (New York residents add appropriate sales tax), payable to *Harlequin Reader Service* to:

In the U.S.

Harlequin Reader Service
Book Rack Offer
901 Fuhrmann Blvd.
P.O. Box 1325
Buffalo, NY 14269-1325

Offer not available in Canada.

BKR-1

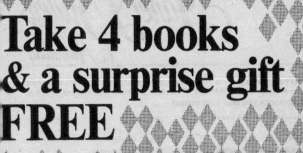

Janet Dailey
Americana

Don't miss a single title from this great collection. The first eight titles have already been published. Complete and mail this coupon today to order books you may have missed.

Harlequin Reader Service

In U.S.A.
901 Fuhrmann Blvd.
P.O. Box 1397
Buffalo, N.Y. 14140

In Canada
P.O. Box 2800
Postal Station A
5170 Yonge Street
Willowdale, Ont. M2N 6J3

Please send me the following titles from the Janet Dailey Americana Collection. I am enclosing a check or money order for $2.75 for each book ordered, plus 75¢ for postage and handling.

_____	ALABAMA	Dangerous Masquerade
_____	ALASKA	Northern Magic
_____	ARIZONA	Sonora Sundown
_____	ARKANSAS	Valley of the Vapours
_____	CALIFORNIA	Fire and Ice
_____	COLORADO	After the Storm
_____	CONNECTICUT	Difficult Decision
_____	DELAWARE	The Matchmakers

Number of titles checked @ $2.75 each = $_____

N.Y. RESIDENTS ADD
  APPROPRIATE SALES TAX $_____

Postage and Handling $___.75___

              TOTAL $_____

I enclose _____

(Please send check or money order. We cannot be responsible for cash sent through the mail.)

PLEASE PRINT

NAME _____

ADDRESS _____

CITY _____

STATE/PROV. _____